To, millie, Enjoy your to Gladstones.

M.J. Manley.

About the Author

I was born in Bath, moved around a lot as a child and adult. I enjoy country and city living, where I find inspiration to do what I love the most... to write. I live in Chelsea, London.

Gladstones

M.J. Manley

Gladstones

Olympia Publishers
London

www.olympiapublishers.com
OLYMPIA PAPERBACK EDITION

A CIP catalogue record for this title is
available from the British Library.

ISBN: 978-1-84897-769-3

This is a work of fiction.
Names, characters, places and incidents originate from the writer's
imagination. Any resemblance to actual persons, living or dead, is
purely coincidental.

First Published in 2017

Olympia Publishers
60 Cannon Street
London
EC4N 6NP

Printed in Great Britain

Dedication

To you three… Harry, Lewis and Isabel. I got there in the end. Love is a powerful emotion.

Acknowledgments

Harry, you found my unfinished manuscript and sat down to read scraps of paper saying, 'this should be published.'
(Antonio Tony) Torino my boyfriend, we have been through so much in the last three years, but you believed in me and said, 'You are a writer.' You encouraged me all the time to write and finish Gladstones.
A big thank you to you both, you both love me very much, but I believe I love you more.

Chapter 1 – In the Beginning.

Doris had worked for Lord Bertie and Lady M. Wakefield forever, it seemed like it was going to be for an eternity. Doris was the backbone to this fine establishment; she had started as girl Friday and worked up to housekeeper, then house manager. Doris became very much hands-on, knowing how his Lord and Ladyship liked the house to be run and Doris fitted in accordingly, making sure that her Lord and Ladyship's every need was met. Being two steps ahead at all times was a must. If they needed extra staff, travel arranged, extra flowers in the drawing room, or a cake to be made for a special occasion, Doris was the person ready to fulfil these tasks.

His Lord and Ladyship lived at a place called Gladstones Manor, taking its name from the very stones the estate stood on, Gladstones. The Manor stood in the most picturesque grounds. The grounds extended as far as the eye could see and stopped just beyond the stones, where the smooth, sharp stones ended the carpeted moor began. Buddy never came here very much, not in the early years as it was forbidden, though she was always allowed to venture out with Betty when it was time for her to go home. They would walk together through the gate that was reached at the far end of the garden, between the wall of the Butterfly Garden and the boundary of the Manor. The gate was very high, and concealed by a high privet hedge which had been overgrown on purpose by the head gardener, but the gate was always kept locked, to keep them all safe and to keep unwanted intruders out! So they would walk through here, known as Gladstones' Side, through Gladstones, and once they reached the beginning of the moor, Betty and Buddy would embrace and say goodbye. Buddy would then make her way back, either on her own or with Glitter. But then she, was never ever on her own really, believe it, because someone was always with her in spirit. Anyway, if she needed Glitter he was never too far away – if she was in danger or just needed some company. It just took a little imagination and he would be right by Buddy's side.

Everybody that came here was totally enchanted by this place, it certainly took Buddy's breath away when she first saw it and did the same to everybody else's breath..

Anyway, let's get back to those stones! "Stones?" Buddy can hear them say. Yes, the famous Gladstones that covered the earth flat like the soil. Yet, for some reason, a few had gathered together like shards of glass pointing bolt upright, like soldiers standing to attention, ready for a guards inspection. This was one of the most famous landmarks, conspicuous, yes, but not to everybody and everything. Hard to believe, but what somebody perceived to be there, others could not always see, even if it was right under their noses or staring them in the face!

Equally, the Manor was exceedingly impressive; it dated back to the early sixteenth century.

An early Elizabethan Manor built in the shape of the letter E. The exterior of the Manor was made of the fine, honey-coloured ham stone, which glowed even more when the sun shone! Inside, the Manor was opulent in every detail, but it was very much a family home and was treated as such.

His Lord and Ladyship were more like family than employers, but Doris never forgot her place and always remained professional, knowing where and when to draw the line.

Doris was married to Horace, who tended to the magnificent gardens. They were so impressive, many smaller gardens within the one whole garden. The garden was divided up into split-levels, with a rock garden, a woodland garden which led into the woods, and a woodland walk. Borders and borders full of perennials that grew year after year. There was the kitchen garden that kept the house filled for most of the year with herbs

12

for eating, but herbs were also grown for medicinal purposes for Buddy, her extended family and her kind. A vegetable garden and a fruit orchard where all the fruit was grown for their consumption and any surplus produce was taken to town to the local fortnightly farmers market to be sold. All the proceeds would later be equally split by Doris and sent to M's favourite charities. Or even to the beggar that was seen on the pavement in town. M just despised the government at times for not doing more for the homeless. It was so very wrong how the government earned so much yet they seemed to turn a blind eye and let this poverty continue day after day.

Buddy had spent endless hours here, playing in the gardens, exploring with her friends – Glitter, Gooey, the family and her extended family, which were always found in the Butterfly Garden and in the woodland. The gardens were formal, yet with so many focal points, including a sculpture of a cast-iron butterfly (she was her favourite), a bare lady made of stone and a summerhouse; they filled you with a sense of joy. It was a fun, intriguing place that was enticing and captivating.

Horace's attention to detail certainly showed, and of course the location of the property always helped. The gardens, which were situated all around the Manor, created a safe haven for them all. With the Manor and gardens combined it looked more like a palace or a museum then a simple family residence. It was just that, a simple family home.

One very special secluded garden could only be entered by the Gladstone side, which was south facing, where the sun always shone. It was the Butterfly Garden, which was filled with scented Gardenias, Ice plant, Buddleias, Michaelmas Daisies which attracted numerous butterflies, The Peacock, Painted Lady, Tortoiseshell, Red Admiral and White Admiral butterfly species were often spotted. Part of the garden had been left as a meadow, and also nettles and thistles were grown in part of the garden to help the Tortoiseshell and Peacock population. Paths led right through the meadow, which then led on to the woodland where brambles grew. This was the White Admiral's favourite source of nectar and their most favourite place.

Horace would also lay out rotting fruit, especially banana skins. All butterflies loved this treat, but the Peacocks loved the rotting fruit the best. Every plant was vetted and double-checked before entering this sacred place, by Horace. Then, once Lord and Lady were happy, the plants were planted – only flowers that would attract the butterflies, and most importantly feed them, were ever planted here!

The other staff who were employed at the Manor included Henrietta, who was a fantastic cook – her food was very scrumptiously delicious. Always left your taste buds tantalized, dancing on ones tongue and screaming out for more. Henrietta likes to be known as Hettie, as she thought Henrietta was rather a mouthful, but Her Ladyship thought this was such a shame as she thought it was such a beautiful name and hated a name ever to be shortened. Hettie was rather a large lady, big arms, big bosoms which you nearly got suffocated in as she gave you a friendly embrace. Some found this a little overbearing but she did not mean to offend, and would have been horrified if she made you feel in anyway insecure when meeting her. With her two big, rosy cheeks and her hair worn in a bun at the back of her head, she was the typical stereotype of an old-fashioned cook, whom you would find in any large, country, family-run residence. Everything about Hettie was big and beautiful, and she had a big heart to match too.

Betty was a general help, wherever she was needed in the Manor. Betty was the only member of staff that did not live on the premises, she insisted there was no need as she only lived a mile away across the moor, just beyond the Gladstones. Betty was happy to go between Doris and Hettie, just as long as she was not in the middle of them. They had their squabbles, but generally saw eye to eye. One would say a love-hate relationship,

Buddy just thought it was a healthy banter between them. They certainly had one thing in common and that was in no doubt, their love for Gladstones. They were so very passionate about their home.

Mr. Simpkins (who was known to everybody as Simpkins), was the handyman, and mended anything that was in need of his toolbox, or anything that needed to be replaced, inside or outside of the Manor. The thing was, once he had checked the whole estate, it was time to start at the beginning and check all over again! Simpkins found this a daunting task but he would not change his life for anything.

The Lord and Lady had been married for several years and had always wanted a large family. The Manor was so large, with a granny annexe, staff quarters and even boasted several beautiful cottages within the grounds. So there was plenty of space for a large growing family.

Unfortunately, it soon became quite clear that there was not going to be the sounds of pattering feet on the flagstones and children's laughter echoing from the great walls of this home. Lady M became a recluse, though the dogs helped; they were her babies, giving her solace when it was needed. This did annoy the Lord somewhat, as to him, they were just animals. Though deep down, they were his boys. He quietly adored these four black Labradors, with their big, black eyes and silky, smooth black coats. They were nicknamed the Magnificent Four, but individually they were called Horatio, Marmaduke, Theodore and Augustine. The dogs had bounds of energy and were walked at least twice a day by the Lord and Lady across Gladstones and beyond, where the moors were. Though they had full run of the gardens – except the Butterfly Garden – the woodland that followed was totally out of bounds to the boys. They were only allowed if they were accompanied on their leads. This was a sacred place. If not, Horace or Simpkins were always on hand, happy to take the Magnificent Four out on their daily saunter, as the dogs always got up to mischief and there was never a dull moment.

If Her Ladyship did not have her dogs beside her, she was always supported by the Lord, who was besotted by her, loved her immensely and would do anything for her. It was not hard to love somebody like the Lady, as she was a beautiful, sophisticated, delightful, charming woman and was great fun to spend time with. Acting normal for her was crazy enough, she had a great sense of humour and was sometimes scatty, but this only happened when she was exhausted and had too many projects on the go. Let's face it, everybody had little quirks (it is what makes everyone individuals and themselves and nobody is perfect. Beings are lucky in life if they find their soul mate and fall in love. Buddy could honestly say though, these two had.

In return, the Lady had so much love to give and she had found her knight in shining armour – the Lord was tall, though slightly overweight (he carried a little too much around his middle). This did not matter in the slightest to Her Ladyship. She loved Bertie for who he was and would not change him for anything.

You would think, with Bertie being slightly overweight, that it could be blamed on Hettie's cooking. In actual fact, the Lord was a very good cook himself and when Cook had time off, which was often, you could find His Lord and Ladyship in the kitchen, cooking their evening meal. The Lord had once said "It's fifty-fifty. If I cook, you clear up," and this worked vice-versa. They had both smiled at one another admiringly. To see this sharing was a wonderful sight, but that was how it was for them, just being. They just seemed to know what each other was thinking and wanted. They were each happy in the relationship, it was not hard; it was the easiest part of their lives, being together. The Lord was a kind-hearted man, very considerate indeed, a hard-working man, who loved the good things in life. He had worked hard, and so why should he not reap the rewards, for himself and for the love of his life, Her Ladyship, and their family.

Chapter 2 – What a day.

It was a bitterly cold, frosty morning, but seeing the sunrise helped Betty, as she knew it was going to be a warm winter's day, once the sun woke itself and all of the beings up. This made Betty smile to herself, as she imagined the delightful rays of the sun shining down on her face and soaking into the depths of her dermis, giving her warmth on this chillingly cold, crunchy morning. Gosh, that ball in the sky was like a giant radiator, a real surge of ultimate warmth from the winter sunshine glowing on her, she thought to herself as she made her way across the moor, her steep incline nearly at a breath-taking end. When she had finished climbing the hill, that she was sure was going to finish her of one of these days, she became warm, due to the energy exerted in her steep climb. She was now out of breath, with a dry, hot throat. The dryness of her throat tickled her pink, but it felt as if her throat was covered in rose thorns with each breath. Having a hot throat was no fun. Gosh, she stood still and tried to regain her breath so as to continue her walk, but try as she might it was no good. Betty wiped her forehead, as she was perspiring profusely, and decided to sit down and have a rest to catch her breath. Now, in Greenlands we would have been doing just that. Betty looked down and marvelled at the scenery before her. Wow, what a truly magnificent place this was, and she thought to herself how lucky she was to live in such an idyllic place. Once she had regained her composure, she got up and wiped herself down, tidied her skirts, and began to walk once again.

Buddy knew it was not a typical day. She could not help Betty then, but she could now if only she were able to go back in time. To Betty it was a typical morning, until she had reached the end of the moor and put her foot on Gladstones. At first it did not even occur to her that the air was full of sulphur that left an awful taste in one's mouth, but it was when she looked down to check the hem on her dress that she noticed the ground beneath her feet. Alarmingly, it was burnt, the grass was burnt. The ground was scorched Gladstone side, and yet on the moor nothing was burnt at all, it was what you would expect at this time of year, full of green heather, though it now looked like it had been dried. Some heather was still in full flower and even some of the evergreen shrub gorse, covered in its needle-like leaves, was in flower: beautiful, small yellow flowers, with their distinctive coconut-perfumed scent. The rest was stripped of its beauty and was forlorn and green, full of anger as she walked past, as the needle-like thorns whipped at her skin. She jumped back in a panic, as she felt herself frown and caught herself looking behind.

This was when it all dawned on her. As she looked out across the moor, it was still a beautiful, crisp winter's morning. As she turned and looked in front of her, facing at the beginning of Gladstones, she gasped and, holding her right hand to her mouth, started to tremble. As she had gasped she had inhaled that ghastly substance, which made Betty start to cough. There was no sun breaking through here, no indigo sky, and it was not a beautiful, crisp winter's day. It was a dull, dank, dismal day, a very bleak, miserable, cold winter's day. This was most peculiar, because Gladstones was south facing and the sun always shone here. She had never ever seen it so sullen. She had not budged an inch, frozen to the spot, but just thought one more time that she would look behind her.

The weather behind her was still a crisp, beautiful winter's morning. But when she looked in front of herself and it was the weirdest, most unusual sight, a bleak winter's morning. How could this be the same day, with such a contrast in the weather?

Buddy knew what had happened, and there could always be a contrast and extremes in the weather.

Should she continue to walk on or go back home? One thing was sure, she could not stand here all day. Maybe the cloud would lift and all would be well later. Maybe there had been a fire? Yes, of course, there would be a simple explanation. A feeling washed over her, 'a simple explanation,' but for some reason she knew that there was not going to be a simple explanation for these weather conditions. Betty knew that something very extraordinarily was about to happen, she had a feeling deep down in her bones. She continued on the path through Gladstones and noticed in front of her something, somebody, and someone on – no, wait a moment – *in* the stone. Buddy knew Betty was trying her hardest to fathom out her thought process and what was happening before her very eyes. It was hard to describe to herself what she saw.

As Betty stared harder and harder still, she could see movement within the stone, yes, the stone was actually moving. It was a movement of rippled effects, like water at the seashore edge. As she stood deadly still, with her mouth ajar, and it seemed she was not even breathing at this point, she was about to witness a very astonishing sight that if she had tried or even dared to explain to anybody she would had been ridiculed so much, nobody would have believed her. Living in a different era, a long time ago, her speaking out as to what she had witnessed would have surely put her into a lunatic asylum.

Suddenly, through the ripples, a face appeared and looked around, as if to check for something or somebody. That was when this thing noticed her, and Betty froze again to the spot. Wondering what was going to happen next, she closed her eyes and prayed. Did she dare to peer out of one eye? She did not know what to do, but one thing was sure, Betty was on her own and had to make a decision quickly and accurately. Whatever decision she made it had to be the right one and whatever she decided she would have to suffer the consequences if it all went horribly wrong. What was going to happen to her? She suddenly had an uncontrollable urge to vomit profusely. The most terrible thought had just entered her head, as she contemplated her fate. She was hoping this being was not hungry and had eaten before it had materialized this morning. She was now praying beyond all hope that it was an herbivore and not a flesh-eating blood-sucking carnivore!

Betty now had an overwhelming feeling of nausea. She put her left hand on her stomach and her right hand to her mouth. She was going to vomit, oh how she hated to vomit, anything but vomit. Betty tried her hardest to hold it in, but the force was beyond her control – she retched and with that the whole contents of her stomach was projected through the air and on the ground in front of her. She was in pain, and vomited until the only thing that was left was the lining of her stomach bile which consisted of sputum. Yuck, and the smell was putrid!

As Betty stood, shaking a little now, she looked for the creature within the stone again. As she stared, she could see the head, shoulders and one arm had appeared. The creature looked at her raised his arm. Betty ducked, but there was no place to hide, and as she ducked, the light ducked too and came straight towards her. It was like a massive fireworks display shooting out of his fingers. As this happened, a bright light moved swiftly from his fingers and headed straight in Betty's direction. Betty looked at this strange, silvery light, which was so blindingly bright she needed to shield her eyes. The light suddenly stopped above her head and, as if it had a mind of its own and was thinking what to do next, it hovered there. Then, as if by magic, it dropped from above her head and encircled her. There was no escape! She turned around and tried to break the wall of light, pushing the light, but the power was intense and hot. She was knocked back to the ground with the force of light and with an excruciating pain coming from her hands she looked at them... the palms of her hands were severely burnt. There was no escape, she was trapped in this wall of burning light!

Betty turned around. She could see the creature working his sorcery, and she pulled herself up using her elbows and knees. As she stood, she felt terribly shaky after vomiting so severely. Looking down at the palms of her hands, she saw that she was suffering from the most appalling burns. She was trembling all over and felt light-headed. She started to shiver because she was cold, and by now in a great deal of shock. Her legs felt like jelly and it was then that Betty fell to the ground with a thud. She must have lost consciousness because everything to her went black.

Betty lay in a deep sleep for hours. On awakening, she felt acute pain in her hands and had such a dry mouth, which tasted like sandpaper. As she opened her eyes, she looked up to the sky and could see that she was surrounded by a cage of stone. The cage started from the ground and must have stood at least six foot tall, but was intricately made. It was a sculpture which was three dimensional, it was exquisite, but it was a cage nonetheless. Now she knew what a wild animal felt like that had been captured against its will.

She looked out of the cage and could just make out the dark figure. It was slumped against the stones, which startled her, and she instantly froze again to the spot. She started to tremble again, wishing she had turned and walked back home when she had had the chance.

The figure was hard to make out, and she screwed her eyes nearly shut to try to make out what it was. It was very well camouflaged, as it appeared to be the same colour as the stones. It was frightfully alarming as it actually looked like part of the stone. Was it human? How could it be after all that had previously taken place? She gulped and swallowed loudly.

What was this thing? A stone creature.

As Betty had gulped, the noise disturbed the creature and its eyes had opened. It occurred to Betty, just how she had been startled, this poor creature was probably just as frightened of her, even more so, as he tried his hardest to hide away from her, almost submerging into the stone as to disappear into it all over again. When it had its eyes closed, she could not see it at all. It miraculously just slithered back and became, well, the stone, actually part of the stone. A frightening sight but an amazing one just the same!

Betty managed to pull herself up. She stepped forward and looked out of her stone cage. For the first time, she heard herself trying to talk, but was coughing and spluttering as she had taken in so many fumes from the sulphur. Her throat was so dry. She could hear herself saying she needed water; she so needed some water to quench her thirst. As if by magic, a cascade appeared at her feet, rising upwards. She blinked several times, unable to believe what she was seeing. As this was happening, though, she thought to herself, *great, she had been burnt, captured and now she was surely going to drown.* She thought of being suffocated and submerged in water. She looked at the figure, which still had not moved, but now was not hiding, just staring at her with a sad, penetrating gaze, a forlorn, eerie stare.

Betty started to scream out to the creature, 'What are you doing to me? I mean you no harm. Why are you persecuting me?'

The cascade flowed right in front of her now and was against her chin. If she had opened her mouth, she would have been able to start drinking. It looked fresh, cool and was soothing against her flesh, so inviting. Betty was so thirsty and she so needed to quench her thirst, but her thoughts were racing and the ifs and whats were becoming ridiculous for anyone to contemplate. Why was she thinking could she trust the figure? What if it was poison and he was trying to kill her? If only she knew. She thought again that it probably was going to poison her leave her for dead or eat her. Oh well, at least she would be dead then and would not feel his teeth biting and tearing at her skin, ripping into her flesh and gnawing at her bones. Betty thought she was going to faint after these thoughts, but were they really her thoughts or really Buddy's? Just when it was all too much, suddenly the creature spoke. If only she knew stone creatures are totally vegans! Buddy smiled to herself now.

'Drink and stop thinking so,' the creature said.

'Why should I, are you trying to kill me? The water is getting too high, I am surely going to drown. Please make the level of water go down,' said an alarmed Betty.

Betty did not know what game this creature was playing, but she did not like his sense of humour one bit, and nor was she going to start to participate in his games. Maybe he had decided that she was not going to be a tasty morsel after all. As if by magic, sure enough her request had been heard and the water suddenly descended until it was knee height. Here the cascade stayed and flowed calmly.

Betty was in shock at what she had just seen and heard. She decided to do as she was told, just in case she would suffer the consequence if she didn't. After all that Betty had been through, she was so thirsty she did not care. With that she braced herself, reaching forward with her cupped hands, and started to collect the water. Betty brought the water up to her lips, which were dry and cracked. First, Betty took tiny sips of water, still wondering if it was safe to drink. She thought to herself that it tasted so good, and then found herself taking big gulps of water, returning again and again to the cascade with her hands cupped.

It was then that she turned and looked at the figure, suddenly realising she was being watched from afar. She heard him talking to her again.

'Look at your hands,' the thing said.

Betty looked down at her hands. They were completely healed. As she looked up again she realised too that her confinement was over, her stone cage had disappeared.

'Why did you capture me and burn my hands? I mean you no harm,' she said.

'How did I know? You are scary. But I am sorry; I needed to know you would do me no harm,' he said.

'What are you?' Betty heard herself say.

'Now you are really having a joke with me, you don't know what I am?' he asked.

The figure started to cough, he seemed very weak.

'Please come to me, I need...'

He coughed and he seemed to be trying to talk but Betty could not hear him.

'Why should I come to you, why should I listen to you? How do I know if you are going to be nice or work some more of your light, magic and sorcery on me?' she said.

'Please, I will not. I had to make sure,' he said.

It seemed now to Betty that he was delirious, talking in gobbledegook.

'Don't remind me, little me doing you harm, right?' she said in disgust.

Betty walked gingerly over to the figure. He suddenly disappeared into the stone again. She was facing him now. Well, the stone which he was in. Betty was shaking all over, she could not control or stop her body from the shakes.

'Please kneel down in front of me and cup your hands together,' he said.

'Look, it would help if I could see you, I mean can you not come out of your stone, I mean the stone?' There was no reply. She carried on kneeling down in front of the stone.

She knelt down with her hands cupped. He was coughing and making whimpering sounds, as if he were in terrible pain. Betty looked down at her hands and the water started to flow into them, yet it did not overflow. An astonishing sight, she peered at the water that came from within the palm of her very hands.

'Please help me to drink. I promise I will not harm you,' he said.

Betty looked up at the being. She was opposite him now, well, opposite the stone he was in. Her hands were filled with water,

25

she held them out to him and stretched out to him so he could drink.

Betty was shaking uncontrollably and the water was splashing from side to side in her hands. Her heart was beating and she felt as if it was going to burst out of its cavity.

'It is all right, I will not hurt you again,' he said from within the stone.

His hands suddenly appeared from within the stone and as he held her hands to steady them, she looked away. He appeared more and more. Betty stumbled backwards, dropping the water because as she saw him emerge it was the most amazing sight.

The whole stone was moving, ripples appeared on the surface and then the motion of movement within the stone became more rapid. Then Betty saw, little by little, this figure emerge and then, there, sitting on the stone, was this being. His gaze was less harsh but how could Betty trust him? Betty hastily stood back in awe. Cupping her hands together again, she felt the sensation of water in the palm of her hands again. Betty looked down into the palms of her hands and was totally amazed – water was coming out of the palms of her hands!

'Here, you'd better drink,' she said.

Betty looked up at this creature with a worried expression.

'How did that happen? You made that happen, didn't you?' she said.

'Water,' he muttered.

Again, Betty did as she was asked and, by cupping her hands together again, the water appeared. As it did, she stretched out towards the creature. He reached out and put his hands around hers, so he could guide her to his mouth. Betty shuddered at the thought of being touched by this hideous creature, but in fact he was very gentle. As he was drinking, she noticed that his hands were large, his fingers long and knobbly. His nails were very long, pointed and dirty. There were bumps all over his hands, which ran down to the fingers. His arms were rather long, slim but muscular, and his head was big too, with a mass of straggly hair. It seemed he had a very short torso and it looked as if he had no legs at all. Gosh, she was aware she was starting to stare, but it was difficult – she had never seen anything like this before. To her, his body was not in proportion at all. She decided that he was definitely not human, (in fact he looked quite troll-like) but he seemed kind and was in need of her help. Even though when they had first met he had been horrid to her, she was starting to understand that he was protecting himself.

Betty decided that now was the time to be brave, and if she was going to help this being (and herself) then she would have to talk to him. Betty felt sorry for this poor scrap, she wanted to help but she was afraid. Besides, what could she do to help this thing?

'My name is Betty, what is your name?'

Betty could hear herself wanting to ask this creature so many questions, "why, what, when and where," but you know curiosity did kill that cat and many more after it.

'I,' he said. He coughed and then tried to sit more upright.

'Let me help,' Betty said.

As she reached out to hold him, he seemed alarmed.

'It's all right, I am here to help you, if you will let me,' she said.

She held onto his left arm and tried to pull him up. He was built solid and she could not shift him but on touch he was very much warmer than she had imagined, though he did feel quite clammy.

'Thank you, you guessed right the second time,' he said.

He talked in a clear, persistent manner but in a very gruff voice, which Betty understood perfectly. Under the circumstances, even she was most surprised.

'Excuse me,' she said.

'When you first saw me, you wondered what I was, whether I was human or a stone creature,' he said.

Betty looked at him in shock. If she had looked in the mirror at that moment her eyes would have looked as if they were popping out of their sockets, with her mouth firmly shut.

'How did you possibly know what I was thinking? That's impossible, isn't it?' she asked.

'Impossible to you maybe, to me I know no different,' he said.

'You mean to tell me you know what I am thinking, you are telepathic?' she said.

'Well no… well yes,' said the stone creature.

With her eyes narrowed, Betty was thinking, and with an anxious expression she was trying to figure out what this stone creature was saying!

'Well no—, well yes—, either you are or you are not!' she exclaimed.

'It can depend on a lot of things – how I am feeling, where I am, and certain circumstances. Look, Betty, put it down to me being a thing, a being, and a creature. Anyway, what category do you fit into?' he asked.

'What do you mean?' she replied.

'Well, are you a thing, a being or a creature?' he explained.

'I am just plain old me,' she said.

'What is a "plain old me"?' said the stone creature, looking confused.

'No, no, that is just merely a saying. I am not a thing, a being or a creature. You mean you have never seen a human before?' she said.

'A human? No, I have not. What is a human?' he asked.

'You are looking at it,' she said, amazed that he had never seen one before. 'Gosh, that is totally amazing, but then I have never seen a stone creature before. So, you are a stone creature?'

'Yes,' he said.

'You have not told me your name yet,' she said.

'Give me a chance, we have been talking about other things. And, come to think of it, you did not ask!' he said.

'But I did ask,' she said, feeling slightly smug that she was one step ahead of him now, but knowing he was always going to be ten steps ahead of any being. There was something about him. 'Sorry, so much to ask, it is hard to know where to begin,' she said.

'My name is Stentorian,' he said.

'Cool, sounds powerful! I have a boring name, Betty.' Then she took a massive deep breath and said, 'So, Stentorian, where do you come from and do you have family? Are there more of you? What happened with the weather here today? How can it be a fine winter crisp day across the moor and for it to be so very bleak winter's day here at Gladstones? And why did you torture me?' asked an out-of-breath Betty.

'Humans talk a lot. Questions, questions and more of them,' he said.

Betty was shocked by this remark, but then looked at Stentorian and realised he was being quite humorous with her.

'I have more questions, but give me a chance and I am sure I will get to the last question, given time,' she said, smiling.

'Evil, evil happened here,' he said.

'Evil?' said Betty.

'Yes, evil that you cannot always see and when it is upon you it can be all so late. Oh, so very late,' he said, looking from side to side.

As he said these words, he looked around, as if to make sure they were not overheard. Betty was beginning to feel this was surreal, that she may be in a dream and in a moment she was going to wake up.

'What do you mean, "upon you and it can become all too late"?' she asked.

'Beware of the sudden change in weather, or a breeze. There is unrest in my land. The Evillitons they are trying to take over Gladstones and the lands where I live, Greenlands,' he said.

'How can they, you said your lands were far away from here?' she asked.

'You have to understand, Gladstones is part of Greenlands. They are forever entwining,' he said.

'Tell me about Greenlands and your kind,' said Betty.

'Greenlands is a beautiful, fertile land where the seasons never change, summer is all year long. My kind are a very gentle breed. Though you think I was torturing you, I was really only protecting myself. I was petrified when I saw you and I have never seen anything like it before in my world. My kind have grown in force in recent decades. The females take a long time to multiply,' he said.

'You mean have babies?' she asked.

'Well, offspring,' he replied.

'Yes, I understand, my mother had difficulty conceiving me and then during my nine months gestation she had to have bed rest nearly all of the time. So it was hard on both of my parents,' she said.

'It only takes you humans nine months to have offspring?' he asked, surprised.

'Yes,' she replied.

'The females take at least two years gestation, then it is hard to know if the offspring has survived to full term, and the labour and birth are not without their difficulties. Once the offspring are born they have to be placed into the offspring cave. They take a long time to develop from offspring – peblets, stonies, stonelets, and then to stone creatures,' he said.

'Wow, amazing!' she said.

'So you can understand why I went to great lengths to protect myself from you. In my world stone creatures take a long time to multiply,' he said.

'Yes, I can. Can you tell me about your family?' she asked.

'My family, yes, my family,' he said.

Those were the last words he said for a while. He became very sad and straight-faced.

Betty reassured him, she was sitting opposite him, and at this point she came up and knelt on her knees, bending forwards to comfort him. How does one go about comforting a stone creature? Betty held out both of her arms. His head fell on her shoulder and it felt so right to comfort him by cuddling him as if he was human and do you know, he sobbed and sobbed and sobbed. No tears with his sob though; he just became clammier and clammier. Betty noticed sticky moisture started to seep out from every single pore of his body.

Well, Betty would have been the first to agree with every being that this was not a nice experience, but come on, what do you expect from a stone creature? Buddy had seen this often, not that she liked to see beings suffer emotionally, but this was one emotion she had missed from home.

Betty did not know how much time had passed since she first set eyes on Stentorian but she started to start to wonder what the Lord and Ladyship would say when she walked into the Manor so terribly late.

'It's all right, you will not be missed,' Stentorian said.

'What do you mean?' asked Betty.

'We must make our way to the Butterfly Garden as soon as possible. We must make haste,' he said.

'You did not answer my question,' she said.

'There is a lot happening here today, your Ladyship is pre-occupied and you are not missed at all,' he said.

'Wait just one minute, how do you know about the Butterfly Garden?' said Betty.

'Where I come from, there are different creatures and beings that live in harmony with one another. The butterfly beings are insects and needed our help, so over the centuries we have united to become a bigger, better force. There is somebody in the

Butterfly Garden that is in need of my help. There is so much to explain but I do not have the time to tell you right now,' he said.

Chapter 3 – Butterfly Garden.

Betty need not have worried so, Stentorian had been right. Betty was not missed at all. So much was happening today and Betty was not the only person, being, creature or insect starting to wish that their day had started somewhat differently.

Her Ladyship, was no different to many beings, she also suffered sometimes with insomnia, and last night certainly had been no different. Tossing, turning, turning, tossing, it was totally bizarre. Even His Lordship had awoken, wondering if he had another woman in his bed! Was somebody trying to tell Her Ladyship something?

'Thank the Lord dawn has broken. Gosh, what a long night that was. I do not think I slept a wink all night,' she said, yawning whilst sitting at her dressing table and examining her dark circles in the looking glass.

'Look, darling, you look so sleepy still, why not go back to bed?' said His Lordship.

'No, I couldn't. I think I could do with some fresh air, Bertie,' she said.

'Well, if you are sure,' he said.

'Yes, I am sure, I think I am going to take a stroll to the Butterfly Garden,' she said.

'I will join you later, I have to go and speak with Simpkins about the new garage doors. Do you know they still have not arrived? I do hope they arrive sooner rather than later,' he said.

Bertie might well have been talking to himself because M had stopped listening a long time ago. She felt an uncontrollable urge to get to the Butterfly Garden. There was a force pulling her nearer and nearer. She was totally unaware of this and the evil that was never too far away. She had not even dressed and was still in her lounge clothes.

On entering the Butterfly Garden, beings were instantly struck by the beautiful scented air that invited them to fill their lungs. As they breathed the air up their nostrils and their senses were refreshed, and beings just wanted to inhale this scent over and over again. The air was filled with the light flowery scented Wisteria, Sweet Alyssum, Chocolate Cosmos (which, with its hint of vanilla, was one of Buddy's favourite scents), Gardenia, Lily of the valley, Jasmine, Sweet Pea, but then Roses were one of the most beautiful fragrances in the world. This garden had every scent imaginable, light tones then heavy tones, Four o'clock, Frangipani would hit our nasal passages later in the evening. Her Ladyship found the air to be so invigorating and felt uplifted after her turbulent sleep the night before. She found herself following the path that led from the solid studded oak gate to the wooded bench at the far side of the walled garden. Her Ladyship sat there taking in the rays of sunlight. Had she closed her eyes and drifted off to sleep, she was not sure. As she stirred and woke up, she thought she had heard a loud fluttering noise. As she opened her eyes, she saw a sight that she was sure would stay with her forever. It certainly was an astonishing sight, a miracle. She did not flinch and was not at all scared. There was a very bright light, and she found herself shielding her eyes.

In front of her stood a beautiful butterfly woman. She had long, black, wavy hair, piercing, beautiful, brown eyes and an equally beautiful pair of silk wings that looked as thin as the finest paper but so strong. They were multi-coloured and the sunlight seemed to reflect through them.

'You came,' she said. 'Good, you remembered our dream.'

'Well, a little, not all of it.'

'It seemed so surreal, I did not know what to believe,' said Her Ladyship.

Her Ladyship smiled at the Queen. The Queen just looked on, showing no emotion. They looked at one another, not at all scared but very much aware they came from two completely different worlds.

'Who, what are you?' asked Her Ladyship.

'You have never seen a butterfly before?' replied the woman with the large pair of wings.

'Well, yes, but not one that stood as tall as me, looked human and spoke. No, I can honestly put my hand on my heart and say no, one has not. Definitely not,' said Her Ladyship.

'My name is Queen Zena. Yes I suppose to you I must look very human but I am not,' she said.

'You are a beautiful woman, with the most beautiful pair of wings,' said M.

'Yes, but I can assure you I am not a woman like you, I am an insect,' she said.

'Why have you come?' asked Her Ladyship.

'You do not remember your dream, do you?' said Zena.

'I remember our meeting here,' said Her Ladyship.

'I need you to help me. In return, you will be fulfilled beyond your wildest dreams,' said Zena.

'What would you like me to do, Queen?' said Her Ladyship.

'Please, call me Zena.'

Zena took M by her hand. She stood up and they both walked together back along the path to where the chrysalis had been hiding. Halfway up the path they turned left, at end of the path, where the Buddleia tree stood, where they stopped and stood beside it. As they looked up, there, on the bough, was a chrysalis. The bundle to Her Ladyship looked like a wasps nest but she was about to have the shock of her life.

Zena flew up, and as she was in full flight she hovered, and with both hands free, gently untied the bundle. Her very own bundle of joy. She cradled the bundle and held it tightly as she flew back to the ground. She faced Her Ladyship and then she looked down and opened up the bundle to reveal a beautiful baby insect, which appeared to be female.

Zena looked up, straight-faced, but it was as if she smiled at Her Ladyship with her eyes. 'Meet my beautiful baby insect, Princess Rose, known as Buddy to all, but one exception. Stentorian will call her Bud. Oh, Glitter too,' she said.

Her Ladyship was totally taken aback. She looked at the Queen and then down at this beautiful baby.

'Gosh, I am speechless. Yes, she is so beautiful. Who is Stentorian?' she said.

'Oh, you will meet him later. A wonderful, delightful creature and my closest Holy Servant ever,' said the Queen.

The baby insect looked constantly at its mother, gurgling with delight and smiling away to its heart's content.

'You will bring her up as your own,' said Zena.

Buddy's hearts sank at this point because she did not want to be anywhere other than by her mother's side, but even then she knew it could not be.

'I cannot do that, she is your baby insect,' said Her Ladyship.

'You have no choice, it is written. And besides, I cannot keep her. She will perish and it is too dangerous for her to stay any longer at Greenlands,' said Zena.

'I do not understand,' said Her Ladyship.

'The Evillitons are getting closer by the day. They do not want the Princess to live and take the throne which is rightfully hers. They want to rule our lands and if there is not an heir to the throne their job will become a lot easier,' said the Queen.

As she spoke, Zena looked up to the sky and it was beginning to cloud over.

Suddenly, there was a loud thud at the far end of the garden gate. Zena quickly covered the baby in its chrysalis' blanket. She looked at Her Ladyship and the colour completely drained from her face. This continued down her body. Where the Queen had been a beautiful butterfly, full of colour, she was still beautiful but was completely white.

'Are you all right, you look very pale? Whatever that noise is, or whatever is behind the gate, has you completely petrified,' said Her Ladyship.

'It is not the noise but the cloud in the sky and how the day is becoming duller by the high hours. We soon will feel sullen. The Evillitons,' said Zena.

'Who are the Evillitons?' asked M.

'Pure evil,' she said, looking Her Ladyship right in the eye.

The noise came again but louder this time, somebody was trying to open the gate. Finally, they succeeded and were now in the garden.

'Quick, we must hide,' said Zena. Buddy began to cry, not for herself but out of fear for her mother.

The Queen blew on her face and she froze in time, which protected her. Then, with her huge wings, she wrapped up the baby insect, herself and Her Ladyship. M suddenly felt herself rising – her feet were no longer on the ground. They were now in the air.

'Oh my Lord, now I am flying,' she said.

They reached the Buddleia tree, hanging amongst the blossom, totally camouflaged as they awaited their fate.

'Please do not worry, you are totally safe and you won't fall out of the tree,' said Zena.

'Gosh, I have hurt my shoulder, that gate was so hard to open,' said Stentorian.

'Are you all right, Stentorian? I would have thought you would have used some of your magic,' said Betty.

'It does not quite work like that. I cannot and do not always have magic to use and after the Evillitons came this morning to Gladstones I used my powers, and then I used some power on you as well. I have to recharge myself before I can use magic again,' said the stone creature.

'How do you recharge yourself?' asked Betty.

'Oh, sometimes it's time, weather, temperature, my favourite food, rest and a good drink of bog bean beer. It could take all of these to recharge me, or just one,' he said.

'Bog bean beer, what is that?' asked Betty.

'You never drink beer? It is the best in Greenlands,' Stentorian said.

'So, dare I ask, and believe me when I say that, but why are we here?' said Betty.

'I am here to meet a very dear friend. I only hope they have arrived safely,' he said.

As Betty and Stentorian walked up the path, Stentorian began to smell the air. Instantly, he noticed the cloud building up in the sky. Time was of the essence, he knew he had to find Zena and he had to do this very soon.

They continued to walk along the path and turned right to where, at the end, they would find the Buddleia tree. In a hushed voice, Stentorian called out, 'Zena, Zena, where are you?'

Inside their cocoon, the Queen could hear Stentorian call her.

'Is that your Holy Servant?' asked Her Ladyship.

'Yes,' she said, straight-faced.

'Look, you have to understand that the Evillitons are very conniving and can just appear without any warning. It can also be confusing as to what the signs of their arrival are.'

'But this can be oh so very late. Once they capture you, I am afraid it is fatal,' said Zena.

'Well, how will you know if it is safe?' asked Her Ladyship.

'Well, I need to wait, wait for his sign. Only a limited number of creatures and beings know the sign,' said Zena.

From inside the butterfly wings they watched, waiting for the sign. What was Stentorian doing? He was pacing up and down.

'Can you see your friend?' asked Betty.

'No, I cannot see her but I know she is near. I just have to give her a sign. Then she will know it is I. Once it is safe, she will come out of hiding,' he said.

'So, what are you waiting for?' asked Betty.

'I am just warming up,' he said.

'Warming up?' asked Betty.

As the stone creature said this, he looked at Betty and gave her an almighty grin, but a grin without a smile, as stone creatures do not smile. They hated smiles. Betty was very straight-faced and did not feel like smiling but at that point she managed a weak smirk.

Stentorian now stood in front of the Buddleia tree and raised his arms up with the palms of his hands facing the tree. Zena saw the sign. It saddened her to see, but it filled her with hope to see images from home.

'What's your friend doing now?' asked Her Ladyship.

'Giving me the sign,' said Zena.

'All he's doing is facing us,' she said.

Betty did not see the sign either, she saw the same as Her Ladyship. This was to protect the secret of the sign.

Zena started to float down from the tree and, as soon as they landed, her wings opened. Betty could not believe what she was seeing and her mouth dropped wide open. At the same time, Her Ladyship looked at the stone creature. What was this thing? It was hideous, gosh, she wanted to close her eyes permanently. What was it? Her Ladyship knew that there was a crisis.

As they faced each other, Stentorian bowed in honour of this almighty Queen.

'Your Royal Highness. An honour to assist you again,' he said.

'My Holy Servant, it is always a pleasure to see you, Stentorian,' she said.

'They could be here,' he said.

'I know we must act quickly,' said Zena.

39

Equally Her Ladyship came to Betty's side and they both asked each other if they were all right.

'Betty, what is that thing? It's hideous, it's a monstrosity, it's shocking and ugly,' said Her Ladyship.

'Please, shh... he will hear you and could be offended,' said Betty.

'Whose side are you on? Where do your loyalties lie?' asked Her Ladyship.

'Your Ladyship, I did not mean to upset or offend you and I can understand how you feel. I felt quite the same when my eyes first met with this strange figure. That's just what I thought when I saw him, but real beauty is not skin deep. Look closer and deeper. You will see a stone creature who is kind, not harsh, who is generous and has such a large heart,' she said.

'Stone creatures have hearts?' she said.

Shrugging her shoulders, Betty replied. 'Well, I don't know, I have not had the time to ask. One thing I am sure of though, he would do nothing to harm us at all. I do know that we are safe and we can trust him, even though we have just met with him today,' she said.

'Betty, you must be delirious, you must have a fever and suffering after all of this excitement.' Her Ladyship took Betty's hand into the palm of her own and patted it. 'There, there, it will be okay. On second thoughts, maybe I am the one suffering with delirious thoughts.' Her Ladyship then raised her hand to her own forehead, to check if she was the one with a temperature! 'Remind me to telephone my GP when we get home. Please, I am finding this day intolerable, I just wonder what is going to happen next,' said Her Ladyship.

'Please try to remain calm,' said Betty.

'Calm, if I was calm it would be crazy and how does one remain so after what I have seen, heard and encountered on this day? What we have been through so far today,' said M, raising her voice, which she really did not do very often.

'Please, Betty, just keep your thoughts to yourself. I would rather be kept in suspense, totally in the dark. That way I will not let my imagination run riot.' Her Ladyship had sat down. They continued to listen to what was said and what needed to be done, and in the same breath tried to work out what was going on. It was like they had been both caught up in a surreal world of a story book, a fantasy of stone creatures, a flying queen and a princess who needed a home.

'Who can I hear?' asked Stentorian. 'Is that my little Bud?' He reached out his arms and Zena instantly passed the bundle to him.

'Oh, you are a gorgeous baby insect and I have missed you so much.' Stentorian held the baby close to him and then, holding her under the armpits, he lifted her into the sky. The love was clear for all to see. Oh if there was no war, no hate, no greed, oh how all the beings would all have lived in harmony, Buddy thought. As Zena looked on, a piece of fine silk fell from her eye. This was a tear. Bud was giggling to her heart's content.

Stentorian could see she had been crying Stentorian bowed and said, 'Your Highness, I promise you I will protect her. I wish that things could be different. Are you sure about this, Zena?'

'We cannot change what has been written, it is forbidden. Yes, I will miss her so very much, but we both know she will not survive. Not even all the magic in the world could protect her from the evil.'

They both looked at Her Ladyship and wondered if she was strong enough for the task in hand, but she was the chosen one. Yes, it was a daunting task, but with their help, Her Ladyship was not going to be on her own. Zena was going to make sure she had all the support she needed. She and Stentorian would never be too far away.

'Why choose me?'

'Sometimes in life, each one of us are chosen, whether we are weak or strong. We can be chosen any time to fulfil a task. We all have our paths to walk along, we all come to the crossroads and we all decide our own fates. Or is our destiny in somebody's control? Though sometimes we cannot decide how our lives are mapped out, it is done for us. It is your time, you have been chosen to fulfil this task.'

'Buddy is not human, but looks so human. How can I fulfil her every need?'

'Yes, I agree, she is not human. Stentorian and I will never be far away. We will always be here to advise you, as and when you need our help.'

At that moment, Stentorian, who was holding Buddy, started to cough and held out his arms for somebody to relieve him of this gurgling bundle of joy.

Zena held her baby one more time, held her to her face and spoke to her so softly. 'Please forgive me. I love you, and one day you will understand why I had to leave you.'

But Buddy would not forgive this, or the Queen.

She then passed her to Her Ladyship, placing her in her arms, wrapping her in the blanket.

'I must flutter. Stentorian, are you well enough for the journey home?'

'Zena, I cannot let you go alone.'

'Stentorian you will stay, to gain your strength. We will have to think of a disguise, so as to not frighten anybody. We do not want beings becoming suspicious.'

Zena had many powers and, unlike the Evillitons (who could become invisible at a moment's notice), she could change beings, objects and places into different things.

'Animal, cat.'

'No, the dogs will chase you, you will be harassed until you drop dead.'

'Ok, object? But what? I know, you will be a silver ball.'

'A ball, don't show me to the dogs.'

'You have to be able to be on guard, protecting Buddy and equally everybody in the family. So you will have to move about the Manor unrecognised. Come on everybody, get your thinking caps on. What arrives with a new baby?

'Betty, you will be the new nanny,' said Zena. Betty held her hand to her chest and raised her eyebrows.

'I do not know a thing about babies let alone baby insects!'

'You will and you will find out that you have a unique understanding of baby insects and infants. You will be a complete natural.'

'When?'

'In time, you will see.'

So with this, Her Ladyship, Betty, Stentorian and Zena all thought about what Stentorian could be turned into. "Toys" said one, "Clothes." said another, and "Furniture." said another.

'Wait! I have an idea,' said Betty. 'Excuse me for being forward, Your Ladyship, but I know your mother past away some years ago. What about turning Stentorian into a granny? Your mother in disguise?'

'I, I really do not think that is one of your better ideas, Betty. I have a bad feeling about this, having my mother back, I mean, Bertie will recognise her straight away.'

'It will be fine, you will all create a diversion and as you explain, he will come around.'

'What, to having his mother-in-law back from the dead? Oh all right.'

'You have to remember Stentorian is only in disguise, it is not really your mother in the Manor.'

'Try explaining that to Bertie,' said M, who was at this point in complete disbelief.

This remark left Her Ladyship somewhat speechless. Somebody else also had reservations on this subject.

43

'Zena, not a dress. Please not a dress – and the underwear, you have got to be joking!'

Zena looked at Stentorian and proceeded to change him from a stone creature to a granny. Betty could not hold her smirk any longer and broke into roars of laughter. She walked up to Stentorian and put her arms around him.

'Life will not be quite the same watching you wear a dress instead of your own attire. It is becoming; it suits you. Remember, beauty is in the eye of the beholder.'

'I must flutter, everybody. Take care, and remember I am never far away.'

'Thanks for my dress.'

As Stentorian said this, he held his dress by the hem and started to dance around, 'I am a granny, I am a granny. Do grannies dance?'

'Yes, but not with so much energy,' said Betty.

'But I have lots of energy.'

'That's okay. My mother had lots of energy. But we will have to teach you how to conduct yourself as a lady.'

'Oh dear, this is going to be fun,' said Betty, giggling. 'After seeing you dance around and walk as if you have a melon between your legs, I can tell this is going to be a riot a minute.'

'So I am going to become a lady?'

'Well, a graceful granny,' said Her Ladyship.

'Yuk.'

Buddy knew Zena was going to leave soon but she could never quite calculate when.' Her Ladyship held Buddy up to say farewell. The three of them stood and looked for Zena but she had gone.

So the decision had been made. Stentorian was going to be disguised as Her Ladyship's mother. Betty had no particular role in the Manor, so she was going to be the new nanny and Her Ladyship to be the mother and Bertie to be father. Though this news was going to be hard to break, where there's a will there's definitely a way. So the scene was set. It all sounded far too normal, too perfect.

Could this be so perfect? Beings all knew what happened when two worlds collided. Was adversity about to happen in both their worlds? Time was surely going to tell. Though one little small problem had been overlooked – introducing Bertie the new father to his adoptive offspring and his long lost mother-in-law.

'Oh dear, oh my!' Her Ladyship was not so sure about this idea... It was surely going to drive her dotty and to complete distraction. But she was eager to please and, like always, went along with the idea just to please everybody else. One of these days, though, she would learn to start to speak up once and for all!

Chapter 4 – Would life ever be the same again?

They had all arrived back to the Manor. It had been a long arduous day, full of astonishing surprises. The events of the day had been amazing yet scary, and had left everybody filled with uncertainty and dread. As they all stood there, they looked at one another, knowing and realising none of their lives were ever going to be the same again. They all looked unsure about what lay ahead of them, but their new lives were only just beginning. In an act of solidarity, they all held each other's hands and jumped into the air.

'There is no going back from this, are we all in?' Zena said.

They all looked at each other now, but Zena was right. The future had been written and they had all been chosen – there was no going back. They all had it in their power to change the future but this had a lot to do with the present day and the colliding of Buddy's worlds. The colliding of her three worlds. 'In!' they all said together.

Bertie had had a very strenuous day and wanted so much to wile away the latter part of the day with Her Ladyship, but as usual his time had been taken up with making sure the estate ran smoothly. He hated this and sometimes wished he lived in a small house with a small garden, though in his heart he knew he belonged here. Besides, if he ever made this decision he would have a riot on his hands, a rebellion!

Life was so very short, and he just wanted a quiet and easy one. He did not like hassle of any sort, just a simple existence. After his tiring day, he had come back and decided to go to the drawing room. On entering he had opened the door to find the

Magnificent Four taking a nap. They had stirred a little, but could smell it was Bertie. Bertie did not want to disturb them too much, but the fire did need to be stoked. So he did this, putting another large log onto the red-hot embers. Then he looked at the dogs, which at this point were stretching, yawning and had their eyes half opened.

'What a jolly good idea, that looks very inviting. I think I will follow suit.' He stretched out, with his arms in the air, and took his first rest of the day. As he lay back into the snug, soft cushions they instantly took on his body shape as he started to relax. As he lay back he could just hear the slight snuffles of the dogs breathing, the crackles from the log that began to be scorched and burnt by the everlasting embers. Oh, this is bliss! Silence is golden, he thought to himself... He closed his eyes and had nearly drifted off to sleep when all of a sudden...

'What the devil is going on, what's that noise?' he said as he sat upright on the sofa.

The dogs, of course, had heard the noise straight away and had promptly jumped up. They all bounded to the door barking and sniffing.

Just before the door had opened, Her Ladyship had quickly pushed Stentorian into the shadows, as she knew instantly what the outcome would be. Nobody had really thought this through, the effect that this discovery would have on Bertie. On opening the door, havoc reigned. It was sheer chaos. The dogs bolted out of the door and encircled the three, Her Ladyship jumped, Buddy did not like the strange noise and cried, and Betty stood there quite bemused. Stentorian danced around Betty continuously, as he had never seen a dog before and was so afraid that he thought he was going to be eaten for breakfast, luncheon, afternoon tea and dinner. Oh, and if there was anything of him left, he was sure he was going to be consumed for supper. Yes, he was sure the dogs would be in for a scrumptious treat, but this was beside the point.

Her Ladyship was holding Buddy with one arm, while with the other she tried her hardest to keep the dogs at bay and away from Stentorian. He was sure they would indulge in their wild pack instincts and their beastly habits.

Faced with their snarling teeth, saliva dripping down their fangs and their eyes bulging, Stentorian was screaming and calling, 'Help, Betty, help!'

The dogs were sniffing him and licking him at first, and then started to bite at his clothes. It was then that he ran and jumped on Betty. Luckily for Betty she saw him coming and held her arms out to catch him. Unfortunately though, with the weight of Stentorian, Betty swayed from side to side, and fell to the ground. With Betty laid flat as a pancake on her back and Stentorian sitting astride her, it did look very, very indignant indeed!

Bertie was becoming even more furious as each minute went by. He could not quite believe what he was seeing. With his arms flapping and waving around in the air, he looked like he was going to take flight into the night, or was certain to blow a gasket. If steam was not coming out of his ears, it soon would be. He thought the scene to be quite obscure and was trying his hardest to instil some sort of normality to this dire situation, but gradually realised that this was an impossible task.

So off he marched, not in a very good mood, to fetch something that surely would make everybody stand to attention. As he walked into the great hall, he could just make Horace out. Horace had heard the noise and was just coming to assist His Lordship when he was asked to drag the dinner gong from the long hall. Bertie was about to make M aware that enough was enough. Suddenly, the gong rang through the Manor with such a force that all the commotion that had been happening stopped. Bertie was certainly deafened by the noise of the gong and now was shaking his head from side to side to try to alleviate the pain he was feeling!

'So, now that I have your complete attention, can somebody tell me what the blazes is going on? I simply hate this impertinence!' he said, shouting. He now had a tremendous urge to go straight upstairs to sleep. It's a filthy night, he thought, with the rain lashing against the window panes. He could hear it was coming down hard as it pounded down outside. It had a soothing effect on Bertie but he had to sort out this fiasco inside before retiring for the evening or concentrating on the sounds of nature that helped him to relax.

Horace stood to the side of Bertie with his fingers still in his ears.

'You blithering idiot, take your fingers out of your ears!'

Bertie was hostile, but in a moment he was sure he would do himself or someone harm. As he now had Her Ladyship, Betty and Stentorian's attention, they all started to speak at once. This just irritated him even more.

'Where's the fire? What an earth is going on? And who and what is that hideous thing on Betty.' At this very moment in time, Stentorian still had his back to Bertie. Betty was now looking over Stentorian's shoulder.

'Betty, where have you been all day? Have you seen the state of yourself, you look bedraggled. Actually, you all do.' When he had said this, he looked at Her Ladyship and then to the baby – where had the baby come from? And who was that on top of Betty? With that remark, Stentorian turned around and Bertie had a double take at his mother-in-law, who at that point was supposed to be in heaven. He stood there shaking, yes, and very much stirred!

He backed into the door, nearly tripping on the top step of one of the opulent drawing rooms of the Manor. On entering the drawing room, he was followed by Horace and the motley crew. Simpkins heard the sound of His Lordship calling for him to bring him some brandy into the drawing room as soon as possible. 'Better make that two bottles,' Simpkins heard, and thought he was hearing things. His Lordship was a social drinker, he had the occasional glass of wine with dinner, but it was out of the question for him to be drinking brandy, especially at this time of the night.

'What the devil is this all about, M? It had better be good.'

'Well, it is difficult to know where to begin.'

'How about the beginning? Seems to be as good a start as any.'

It was at that moment their smiles had been wiped completely from their faces.

They had all settled in the drawing room in front of the fire. Simpkins had arrived with the brandy, which Bertie had consumed in one gulp, coughing and spluttering.

'Simpkins, something tells me it's going to be a long night. You'd better bring another bottle.'

'Sir, are you sure?'

'No, but bring it anyway.'

Bertie sat on one sofa and Her Ladyship, who was holding Buddy, sat beside him. Stentorian and Betty were sitting on the sofa opposite him.

'It's not what it seems,' Her Ladyship and Betty blurted out at once.

With raised eyebrows, Bertie started to speak in a whisper.

'Oh, I see. I would like to know how you can possibly tell me it's not what it seems? You're right about that, M, you are driving me dotty, I appeal to you... I am staring at my mother-in-law, who passed away a decade ago. Your,' he spluttered again, screaming at the top of his voice, ' Simpkins, Simpkins, the brandy!'

Simpkins wondered what the gracious was happening, and nearly dropped the brandy onto the floor.

Bertie would have jumped up to collect the brandy from Simpkins but he would have had to pass the mother-in-law as he made his exit from the room. This was not normal, not natural and was not happening.

'Sir, sir, I am here, don't panic.'

'Don't tell me not to panic! How you can tell me not to panic?'

'Sir, you are hysterical. What on earth is wrong?'

With that, Bertie grabbed the bottles of brandy from Simpkins and filled his glass to the brim. Then, he asked Simpkins to turn and see who was sitting on the sofa.

'Bottoms up.'

Nobody could believe what they were seeing. Stentorian held onto Betty's arm and whispered into her ear.

'Don't tell me I am having my first experience of the inside of a loony bin, a mad house.'

Betty was just as surprised as Stentorian, if not more. She had never seen His Lordship act in such a manner.

'No, His Lordship has never has been known to drink so.'

'Steady on, sir, really it surely cannot be that bad.'

'Yes, it can.'

Not taking his eyes off what he thought was his dead mother-in-law, he grabbed Simpkins by his collar and, shaking him, said, 'Don't you recognise the old girl.'

'Less of the old girl.'

'It talks!'

'Bertie, please.'

Both men had turned and were no longer facing each other but were now looking at the mother-in-law that should have been tucked up nicely in her coffin six feet under.

'No, sir.'

'Man, look a bit closer.'

'Oh my, what the devil is going on?'

'Devil, yes it certainly is the Devil's work. Go get some garlic bulbs from the pantry, Simpkins!'

Simpkins had recognised the mother-in-law, and he too had turned deadly white. He grabbed Bertie's arm and would not let go.

'There, there, old chap. Steady on, take it easy.'

'Can it really be?'

'It looks like you need this.'

'Thank you, sir. I have never needed a brandy so much.'

Bertie managed to prize Simpkins hands off his arm (it was like prizing a limpet of a giant rock), only for it then to be replaced by his other. Both men sat on the sofa, huddled together like two lost boys, lost in their deepest, darkest thoughts – wherever that might be, it's hard for Buddy to describe to everyone as she was a girl insect. So there they were, drinking their brandy. Not taking their eyes off this figure that had shared their lives a decade ago. A decade had passed since her burial. They just could not believe it, could they really be staring at the ghost of his mother-in-law? God rest her soul, pray she was resting in peace but this was just not conventional.

'Now, I am sorry, it has been a dreadful shock. I can explain, but please stop looking like a wounded spaniel.'

Both Bertie and Simpkins just sat and stared.

'Are you both coherent?'

They both nodded and had another brandy. Stentorian thought this was highly amusing and decided he would have even more fun. At that point, he started to make himself float, as if he were a ghost. The thing was Her Ladyship could not see what was going on because she was now standing with her back towards Stentorian. Bertie was trying his hardest to concentrate, but he found this unbearable. He got a cushion and hid his face.

'Bertie, what has got into you? You know sometimes things are not always as they seem.'

With that, Her Ladyship looked behind her and Stentorian was sitting pretty, as if he was a proud new grandparent. As soon as Her Ladyship turned back around, however, he was up to his tricks again and had disappeared altogether. Soon he was lifting objects, and really making Bertie and Simpkins' imaginations run riot!

As soon as Bertie and Simpkins saw this, they looked at one another and simultaneously turned their gaze to the empty brandy bottle.

'Oh, well it's either the brandy or...'

'Sir, are you seeing what I am seeing?'

They both screamed, 'It's a... a ghost!'

'Would you two be sensible for just one moment? It's not a ghost, it's Stentorian in a disguise.'

Betty was in fits of laughter, nearly wetting herself. Stentorian had not had such excitement in a long time, Bertie and Simpkins thought they were in heaven and Her Ladyship thought enough was enough. Then, when she realised what was happening, she certainly did see the funny side.

'Look, my darling, are you going to tell me what on earth you think is so funny about having your dead mother on our sofa? I really do not have a sense of humour about this and nor should you.'

'Okay, I am sorry, I will stop laughing and the three of us, Betty, Stentorian and I, will tell you our stories of how we came to be standing outside the front door.'

'Are we all in?' we all shouted together.

One by one they told their story. Bertie and Simpkins were totally mortified by what they heard and at times thought they were in some sort of dream.

In a slurred voice, Bertie said to Simpkins, 'You'd better go and fetch another bottle.'

'Right you are, sir.'

'No more drink, you have had quite enough already.'

They did not believe it and would not have if Stentorian had not called for Zena.

Suddenly, there she was at the door of the drawing room…

'You called?' she asked.

With that, Stentorian jumped down and bowed, 'Your Holy Servant awaits your comment, Zena, my Queen,' said Stentorian.

'Rise, my Holy Servant,' said Zena.

'So, you do not believe, Bertie. Now do you believe?'

Bertie's mouth was so wide open that it looked like he might catch the odd fly.

'Let me close your mouth. Believing is seeing but sometimes I think you need to listen to a story and believe.'

'What, even if they sound so far-fetched?'

'Yes, Simpkins.'

'You know my name!'

'I know you all here at Gladstones. There is nothing that I do not know; well, almost nothing.'

'So, Stentorian, lets change you back to yourself.'

Zena spun her magic all over him. It was fine silk threads that came out of all of her eight fingers and two thumbs. With each thread that touched him, it revealed his true self. When she had finished, both men were standing with their mouths ajar, unable to speak.

'Good to have you back, friend. Come here and give me a hug.' Betty squeezed him tight.

'Steady, Betty, you will squeeze out all my pusses.'

'Oh sorry,' she smiled at him. He looked at her. A friendship had been made today and nobody was to come between these two ever again.

'Oh, yuck, it's disgusting.'

'Why is Stentorian disgusting, because he is a stone creature?'

'You want to take a look in the mirror sometime yourself, it's not very pleasant either.'

'Bertie, please have an open mind.'

'But he's hideous, a stone creature and full of puss.'

'Well you are full of blood, fluid and waste.'

Now, now, we must all come together for the sake of our futures. Does it matter what we beings look like, what our insides are made of? Surely it is our thoughts and the love for each other that counts?' Zena was not worried about Bertie's outburst, it was delayed shock. Nothing that could not be rectified.

They realised though, that when Zena appeared from nowhere and changed Stentorian into his handsome self, a stone creature, they had no choice in the matter.

And they started to believe in the astonishing stories and all the commotions. They too knew their lives would not be the same again but did not have the same enthusiasm as M, Betty and Stentorian. After drinking all of that brandy, their heads were thumping and they were certainly not going to jump up in the air and shout, 'IN.'

'Darling, where is a bucket? I think I am going to vomit.'

'Oh no. Simpkins, quick think of something.'

'Oh, sir, I told you not to touch the brandy, it does not like your stomach at all.'

'Quick, the coal scuttle, yuck.'

'Well, if you must overindulge, what do you expect? But I understand totally under the circumstances. I apologize for all of the grief. I would have done the same thing. Oh, Betty, I am sorry.'

Her Ladyship looked at her beloved husband pityingly.

'It is time for Zena to change Stentorian back into my mother.'

'No, anything but changing him into my mother-in-law, please.'

'How about if Stentorian stays as himself?'

'Betty, we have already discussed this and we all know it would not work. You remember how you reacted, how you all reacted, when you first saw Stentorian.'

'Well, yes it was a shock when you first saw him, but then you realised he was not going to do you any harm.'

'Well, let's have a vote. Raise hands, antenna, wands and rattles. Who would like Stentorian to remain the same?'

Well, the vote was unanimous.

'So, Stentorian stays as he is, his original form.'

Buddy felt a void and Zena had gone again. She hated this when she left.

Chapter 5 – Getting Organised.

Gone were the days when one could get a decent night's slumber. On meeting his new offspring, Bertie had embraced fatherhood with gusto, barely remembering what life was like before his bundle of joy had arrived. Well, this was not entirely true – he missed normality at times. But even when he scratched his temple and wondered what normality even was anymore, looking down at Buddy in her crib, he would not change anything. He knew there was going to be trouble and strife ahead but even that could become a doddle. It just depended on how one looked at certain situations. One of his greatest chums had said: 'Bertie, there is a solution to everything.' He smiled warmly to himself, but then his smiled disappeared as memories of his friend, who had been an up and coming scientist, dying of a disease while working in the field,
flooded his brain. His friend had never been happy with what he had, and greed, Bertie was certain, had killed his dearest chum in the end. He had the wife, the great family, the property, the toys, the cars, but he just kept on working. Why, when there was no need to work and gain a higher bank balance? Anyway, looking at his beautiful daughter, he certainly thought there was a lot to be said for sorcery!

And what a change he had seen in M! She had changed overnight, and was blooming in every way possible! He was the luckiest man in the world. Her Ladyship was so happy and contented and in turn, if his wife was happy then so was he.

He remained happy, even though this new life was fraught with strange sights and looked set to be a never-ending battle. To get through this, everybody took each day as it came. If something strange happened, everybody took it in his or her stride – there may be a discussion occasionally, and this would be the only way some sort of normality was going to keep his or her feet sometimes firmly on the ground!

'You are beautiful.' As he said this to his daughter he poked her tummy with his finger. Buddy giggled and Bertie smiled back. Her Ladyship was stirring.

Lots of things had change. One thing which stood out was Stentorian's hatred for anything that was magnetic! Everything magnetic had been removed from within the Manor and even from the grounds outside. Stentorian had been strict and had said it attracted evil and it was to protect Bud.

'Come on, time to get you up. Stentorian will be here soon with your nectar milk. So, come and see mummy first.'

'You lay there.'

'Good morning, Bertie.' He got a big kiss planted on his lips and a big hug.

'M, that felt so good.'

'It did.' She kissed him again, and they would have got carried away totally if it had not been for the knock on their bedroom door.'

'Oh no, don't answer, Bertie.'

'Believe me, I do not want to. This will keep until later.'

'I hope not too much later.' They both smiled at one another.

'Good morning, you two. Come on in.'

Her Ladyship had sat up in bed with Buddy on her lap.

'Good morning, Stentorian. Good morning, Betty. And what a delightful one it is too.'

'Good morning. And how is my little Bud this morning?' asked Stentorian, as he walked up to Buddy.

Once Buddy had seen him, she started to flap her arms and legs as if she were a beached seal or whale marooned on the beach. She squealed with delight and smiled from ear to ear.

'Well, I think we can safely say that Buddy is delighted to see Stentorian. It is joyous to see and hear,' said Bertie.

'Good morning. Did you all sleep well?' asked Stentorian.

'Yes, thank you,' said Her Ladyship.

After the incident of meeting Stentorian, everyone had agreed he should keep his own appearance. Yes, it had taken some time to get used to but it was in the interest of Bertie's sanity, and as Stentorian had pointed out, he felt the same about them. As much as they thought he was hideous, he found humans to be even more so. So, it was agreed. And more importantly Buddy had to get used to growing up with a sense of consistency.

In her world, seeing a stone creature floating past, popping up here and there, was so very normal. It would have been depriving her of a normal chrysalis-hood.

'Here is the nectar milk,' said Stentorian.

Buddy was fed; she drank her feed with delight and had finished in no time at all. She hated it when Her Ladyship took her petal bottle away.

'Stentorian, do you think Buddy needs more? She seemed to finish her feed so promptly.'

'I will increase the volume but not yet, the time is not right. If she has too much too soon it could have dire effect.'

'In what way?'

Stentorian looked around the room at them all.

'You don't know, do you?'

'Know what old chap? I mean, old stone.'

His face was rigid and he took Buddy from her Ladyship's arms and held her close to his chest, as if to protect her from herself and the two colliding sinister worlds.

'You are scaring me, what is it?'

'If Bud is given too much feed during her delicate development she will surely die, a drop too much will kill her. Do not ever be tempted to give in to her. She will make you think she wants more but believe me, she is full.'

Their faces said it all – they did not know how to console themselves.

59

'This is terrible!' they all said together.

'Please do not worry so, it is just one part of Bud's development. In time you will all get used to Bud's needs and what she will need as she grows.'

'Betty, could you please wind Buddy while I run my bath?' asked M.

Betty noticed it first because she knew that she would never, ever forget the smell. She saw that Stentorian had become irritable and was not really concentrating.

As Betty held Buddy, she looked at Stentorian. She did not even have to ask him what was wrong. It was the smell that she would never forget, sulphur.

'Stentorian, they are here, it's the Evillitons. I would recognise that smell anywhere.'

'Everybody, get down and stay there.'

Betty was facing Stentorian now. 'I am very scared.'

Stentorian put his hands onto Betty's arm to comfort her. He looked at Bertie and Her Ladyship.

'What's going on?' asked Bertie, alarmed.

'No time to explain. Just get down and take cover,' instructed Stentorian.

Stentorian looked at Betty and looked back out of the window. Suddenly, the impact threw him into the air with an almighty force. It was so overpowering, it was as if a tornado had ripped through the bedroom, leaving the bedroom looking like an empty shell. It was the magic from Zena that made Bertie, M, Stentorian, Betty and Buddy survive the attack from this evil force. This was what your worst nightmares are made of: this was evil at its worse!

Evillitons could not always be seen, but they could always be smelt. When beings were unlucky enough for them to show themselves it was a very unpleasant experience indeed. Or sometimes, if beings were terribly unlucky, they would just have a feeling, a sense that they were there. Sometimes beings could see the evil in front of them which was a very unpleasant experience. When the almighty force of their wind engulfed you, you were powerless against the strong magnetic force. There was sometimes a dramatic change in the weather as well, but again this notice may come all too late.

Bertie and M looked on helplessly, while Betty held tightly onto Buddy and was not going to let go.

The wind pushed against the bedroom windows, shattering them. Everybody turned away from the flying glass, praying and hoping it would not hit them. Stentorian was picked up by the force and was thrown hard against the wall.

Betty turned and looked at Stentorian, worried for his safety, but before she had time to even move, the evil encircled her and Buddy.

Betty started to scream. The force of the wind was so powerful that she found herself being pulled closer to the windows which led out onto the balcony.

The Evillitons tried to pull Betty and Buddy off, through the opened window.

But they could not. Betty hung derterminedly to the bed, one arm still clasping Buddy to her chest, resisting the force with all of her might. This only made the Evillitons more determined. And when they did not get their own way beings had better watch out, their temper was vicious.

Zena had created her very own wall of defence. Her cold breath blew onto Buddy's face and her body, freezing her in time and protecting both herself and Betty. Evil could not penetrate the wall, and Evillitons hated the cold.

As soon as they felt the cold, they left. But they were not going to be defeated that easily. They would be back, that was for sure!

Doom and gloom filled the room with a fog so thick you could write your name in it.

'Stentorian, are you all right?' asked Her Ladyship.

Her Ladyship helped him up and he promptly took Buddy from Betty and laid her on the bed.

'We need to take Bud to the Butterfly Garden straight away.' Bud was coughing and it was distressing to hear and see.

Betty too sat on the bed, and seemed dazed by her first encounter of the Evillitons, but it was Buddy that was concerning Stentorian. She seemed to be getting very distressed by her coughing.

'While we are in the garden I need you, Betty, to collect this list of flowers for me, while I make a potion to help Bud, who has inhaled too much sulphur.'

'Can we not give her a sip of water?'

'No, darling, remember what Stentorian said.'

'Oh, this is too much to bear.'

Bertie comforted M, but this had really scared her and she too was still coughing from the putrid air that had engulfed then all.

'I am fine, do not worry about me. Are Buddy and Betty all right?' asked Her Ladyship.'

Buddy was well, it seemed at the time, perfectly fine, and so was Betty, but what would happen the next time they encountered the Evillitons? They might not be so lucky.

'While we are all in the Butterfly Garden, we must all be vigilant. Bud will be fine, I am certain, when she is in the fresh air, but this is something she will have to get used to. In time as she grows, her lungs will go from strength to strength. One day she will cough no more.'

As Stentorian walked over to the broken bedroom windows and looked out across the garden, he could see the blue sky had returned and knew the evil had gone. The fog too was lifting from the bedroom.

'Look, everybody', he said, 'the evil has gone.'

Everybody walked gingerly over the broken glass and wood to gaze out at the beautiful day that was unfolding now that the evil had disappeared.

'Look at all of this mess,' said Her Ladyship.

'The room will be transformed by the time you arrive back,' said Stentorian.

'What do you mean transformed?'

'M, I think you should put more faith and trust in what Stentorian says.'

'I do, Bertie, but it is just taking a little time to adjust to Stentorian's world.'

'I know,' said Bertie, placing his arm around M's waist to comfort her.

'You are doing well. You would had never been chosen if we did not think you could cope, but we do know it is going to take you time to totally be at ease with what you see and, believe me, you have seen nothing yet,' said Stentorian.'

'Come on,' said M, 'time for some fresh air.' So they all headed to the garden.

'Come on, Stentorian let's race each other to the gate,' Betty laughed jokingly.

'We will see about that!' As Stentorian said this, he winked at Betty and gave Bud a look… It was as good as a being's smile.

They all walked down to the garden, well, Stentorian did not walk, he hovered, His Lord and Ladyship hand in hand, giggling at one another and never missing an opportunity to be flirtatious. Stentorian could hover very quickly. With their very short legs, Betty could understand why stone creatures were made to hover and not to walk, it made perfect sense.

Let's also remind all beings where Stentorian came from. He did not always hover, and where he came from if he felt like appearing then that is exactly what he would do. Stone creatures and beings, and like them could just appear where they wanted, that was normal. Walking was not!

Betty did not mind this, as she hated to walk. With Buddy on her back this was ideal anyway. She would put her arm into Stentorian's as they walked/hovered along together and chatted about Buddy, Greenlands and, of course, Gladstones. There was always something to talk about. Stentorian also had to rest, as his frame was not built to hover continuously.

'I thought you were going to race me to the gate?' joked Stentorian.

'It's such a beautiful day, it seems such a shame to be in a rush,' said Betty.

And with that, pop! Stentorian was gone, leaving Betty stunned at what she had just seen!

Bertie and M had gone on ahead, but had looked back and decided to walk back to where Stentorian and Betty were.

'Did you see that? You must have just seen that, surely?' said Betty to Bertie and M.

They both looked at one another, then back at Betty, and said together.

'Saw what?'

Betty started to shake her head from side to side, looking over the shoulders of her employers.

'Stentorian. He must have passed you.'

A big, deep laughter came out of Bertie's mouth.

'What is so funny?'

'The look on your face. Stentorian is working his magic again,' said Bertie.

'But he was here one second and in a blink of an eyelid he disappeared. He has completely vanished into thin air.'

'Have I, though?' said Stentorian, as he stood in front of Betty.

Betty jumped out of her skin.

'How did you do that?' asked Betty.

'Betty, sometimes it is better for one to observe than to try to work out the ins and outs of one piece of sorcery,' said Bertie.

'It's all in a blink of an eye,' said Stentorian. Looking, he said he had been waiting for Betty at the gate. 'After all you did say we were going to have a race.'

'Well, what I was about to discuss with you, Stentorian, really does not have to be discussed anymore,' said Bertie.

'What?' asked Stentorian.

'Well, I did not realise you could pop here, pop there, and get around so quickly. I was going to suggest a little help with one's walking, but no problem – you also hover!'

Stentorian looked on with bemusement but was eager to hear more.

'Well, after a while the hovering does get tiring too. But do go on,' said Stentorian.

'Yes,' said M and Betty together.

'Well, I was going to talk to Simpkins about making some sort of device,' said Bertie, as he watched Stentorian hover painstakingly down towards the garden.

'Here, here, what a good idea, darling. What do you say?' asked M.

'What type of device are we talking about here?' asked Stentorian?'

'Well, I was thinking about some sort of trolley, but you don't need it anymore, as you can move very swiftly,' said Bertie.

'Well, Bertie this is not such a bad idea. I cannot use my powers all the time so, yes, please continue. But the trolley would not work because then somebody would have to push me. I need to be independent,' said Stentorian.'

'What about a train mobile?' asked Bertie.'

'What?' everybody said in unison, their faces the picture of confusion.

'By jove, I've got it – we will get you a buggy.'

65

'A buggy, what is a buggy?' asked Stentorian, looking somewhat bemused.'

'A small, lightweight vehicle. The type of vehicle that I have for when I play golf. It takes me all over the course very quickly, enabling me to play a longer game. Also, I can use it to carry my golf clubs and other equipment that I need for my game.'

'Well, yes, I will try,' said Stentorian.

'I will speak to my supplier and get one customized for you,' said Bertie.'

'Okay. I will look forward to this vehicle, but you will have to teach me to drive,' said Stentorian.

'Drive,' said Bertie.

'Well, yes, I do not know how to drive,' said Stentorian.

M and Betty laughed. This was something they would definitely have to see. This was going to be such fun. For who, that was the question.

'No problem, I will have you driving in a week.'

'A week, Bertie, are you sure? This is an event not to be missed, I wait in anticipation.'

'You and me both, darling!'

'You do know what you are doing, don't you Bertie?'

'By jove, of course, Stentorian, have faith.' He put his arm around Stentorian, though he did not know at this point who needed to be comforted more, Stentorian or himself. What had he got himself into? Oh well, a fun week was going to be had by all. It would not be at all surprising if the laughter was accompanied by a few painful bruises and bumps!

They entered the Butterfly Garden, and M untied the cloth that secured Buddy onto Betty's back, holding her in her arms.

'Now, you must all stay here while I scrutinize the garden and make sure it is safe for Bud and us.'

Pop! Stentorian was gone. Gosh, they all thought, how amazing it was how Stentorian would come and go so quickly.

'All is clear,' Stentorian said, making everybody jump out of their skin as he popped back in an instant.

'Stentorian, it would help if we could see you,' said Betty.

Pop! Stentorian's face appeared and Betty was totally in awe of him. Betty realised Stentorian's sorcery was very powerful and was in no doubt that she had not seen all that he could achieve through it.

'Here I am,' said Stentorian, as he now faced Betty. Betty looked behind Stentorian's face to see if she could see the back of his head. It was amazing, she could see nothing! This was incredible magic.

'How do you do that?' asked Betty.

'Years of practice. Remember, it is in my genes,' said Stentorian.

'Truly amazing, unbelievable, is it not, M?' marvelled Bertie, shaking his head.

'Well, yes,' said M. But Her Ladyship was still getting used to the idea of seeing Stentorian's magic, which at times left her feeling slightly uneasy. She did not know what was real anymore and was finding it hard to adjust to this world of sorcery!

'Stentorian, can you teach me to do some sorcery?' asked Bertie.

'No, I cannot teach this to anybody! Remember, I was born with my powers. They are very powerful – it took me a long time, great courage, to decide to use them. I also had to teach myself how to be in control of this great mastery.'

'Yes, but did your parents never teach you?' asked Bertie.

'Well, teach is the wrong word. In my world you are shown from a very early age to respect the sorcery that has been bequeathed to you first. Then, and only then, will the magic show itself to you. Then you must decide how to control the power that is within you as an individual, and know when to use it and not to abuse it.'

'You have to promise me, Bertie, never ever to dabble in any sorcery. It can be very dangerous and does not always go the way you intend it to! It can have devastating effects on whoever dabbles in it. Beware! The Evillitons are trying to find the Tome to increase their knowledge of sorcery,' said Stentorian.

'What is a Tome?' asked Betty.

'It is a large book,' said Bertie, glancing at Stentorian and wondering what this book was, and why it was so sacred.

'The Tome is full of spells that date back thousands of years, tried and tested by past and present generations. We hope—' said Stentorian.

'Who are "we"?' asked Betty. 'Sorry to interrupt.'

'Our kind, stone creatures, beings and of course the butterfly beings. We hope the Tome can be preserved and not be touched or used by the wrong creatures, beings and people. One day, Bud will need to learn the whole Tome to ensure the spells gain strength and live on through the next generation and many more future generations.'

'How will she learn? It sounds a daunting task,' said her Ladyship, looking down at this baby who did not realise her fate.

'She does realise her fate, even now,' said Stentorian.

Her Ladyship looked up at Stentorian, speechless, and her mouth was totally agape.

'What's wrong, darling?' asked Bertie.

'I cannot believe it,' said Her Ladyship.

'Believe what?' asked Bertie.

'Stentorian is telepathic.'

'Well, nothing would surprise me about Stentorian,' said Bertie.

'Is it true?' they both asked, looking at Stentorian.

'Yes, it is true, but I don't have this power all the time,' said Stentorian.

'So, how does Buddy realise her fate at such an early age?' asked Her Ladyship.

'She realises that she is a very special baby. Before she came out of her chrysalis, her life flashed before her eyes and so she realises the daunting task that lies ahead of her. But she does not know everything,' said Stentorian.

Bertie, M and Betty were totally amazed at what had reached their ears. They looked at one another in bewilderment, then stared in amazement at Buddy and Stentorian in turn.

'Is she frightened?' asked Betty.

'No, because she will be brought up with the knowledge of how she will deal with her daily tasks, and she will know her goals in time. She will learn, but her lessons will be hard. It will not be easy, I admit, but together we can make sure she has a solid foundation on which to build.'

It was beautiful down in the Butterfly Garden. The sun was shining and there was breeze which kept everyone cool. Betty had collected eucalyptus, which grew native to Australia but also grew beautifully in the Butterfly Garden, lungwort, oregano and thyme, so Stentorian could prepare a tea; the little leaves packed a potent punch for any cough. Feverfew, which Stentorian used in herbal medicine for headaches, was picked too. The various flowers requested by Stentorian were placed in a trug, ready for his use.

'Pucker up, Bud. Here, suck a lemon' said Stentorian. This had definitely helped Bud's cough. As well as helping Buddy's cough subside, the fresh air was actually making everybody feel a lot better.

'Watching our daughter suck a lemon certainly reminds us all that she is definitely not human, but a very special being indeed,' remarked Bertie.

'Is everyone ready to leave? I feel that Bud needs a nap,' said Stentorian.

'What a splendid idea,' said M.

'It's all right for some,' said Betty. Knowing Bertie and Her Ladyship, they were also going to take advantage of Buddy's nap time and have a sleep themselves.

'Credit where credit is due, Betty, you have been wonderful since Buddy arrived,' M said happily.

'Sorry, I hope I wasn't being too forward,' Betty said with a smile.

'We know exactly what you mean,' said Bertie, smiling also.

'No, seriously, if you wish to have a lie down while Buddy is taking hers then, by all means, please take one. If you are still asleep when Buddy wakes, I am sure Stentorian will step in and assist her.'

'Of course, you do not even have to ask. You know that,' said Stentorian

'Well, I do not know what to say.'

'I would strike while the iron's hot,' said Bertie.

'I do not need to ask for anything else,' said Betty.

'Say nothing. Really, there is no need' said Bertie.

'Before you have a nap or a sleep, Betty, I need you to help me in the kitchen,' said Stentorian.

'Watch out. I do not think Hettie will take kindly to her kitchen and pantry being in disarray. Especially with tomorrow being a very special day,' said Betty.

'No, and I certainly do not want to be in the firing line when Hettie gets cross. I can see her now, her face purple with rage chasing you around the big, long kitchen table with her rolling pin in her hand. Hettie would have you for breakfast! When she gets cross, it is good to be a million miles away.'

'I agree, that is no consolation. But please remember, Hettie has been working extra hard because of tomorrow. I have asked her to have a rest this afternoon. She is actually going to take the afternoon off,' M said, as she prepared Buddy for her nap.

'Betty, you make her sound like an ogre. Except she is a woman, of course.'

'Stentorian, you have to remember the kitchen is Hettie's domain, but she is a kind person. Just do as you are told in there or we will hear about nothing else for months to come,' said Bertie, smiling, with a twinkle in his eye, at Her Ladyship.

With that, Bertie held Buddy. 'Say goodnight to your Stentorian.'

'Goodnight, little one.' And he stroked Bud's cheek with his long, knobbly finger. 'I will leave you now,' he said, and kissed her on her forehead.

Buddy reached for his finger and clasped it for the first time. This amazed Stentorian, as already her grip was strong and she was still not quite a year old. Both Bertie and Stentorian thought how sweet this was.

As Stentorian left, another thing that both human and creature noticed was that Buddy cried for the first time. The sobs were pitiful, and as Stentorian got further away they became worse and worse.

M opened the bedroom door. 'What is the matter, Buddy?' she asked, trying to console her.

As Stentorian reached the end of the corridor, he turned and wondered whether the time had come to test Buddy's powers. He tried to speak to Buddy telepathically, unsure if Buddy could communicate with him like this yet, or even if she would ever be able to. Nobody knew yet what Buddy was capable of, but there was only one way to find out.

'Why do you sob so, little one? Please stop weeping.'

'You are going to leave me now,' said Buddy.

'That's amazing, the sobbing has stopped,' said Bertie and M together.

Amazed at this milestone, Stentorian hovered up the hallway back to Buddy, who was still in Bertie's arms, outside of his bedroom door, with M.

'What are you still doing here?' asked M.

'It was Buddy and her sobbing. I could not bear it. Can I hold her?'

'Why, of course. You never have to ask, old stone,' said Bertie, looking a little puzzled.

Stentorian reached for Buddy and held her under her armpits with his arms up into the air. He spoke to her telepathically.

'I am so sorry, please forgive me, I never meant to make you weep so. When I said I was going to leave you now, I meant only while you were sleeping, my little Rosebud.' He brought her back down and held her close to his face. Then, she spoke to him once more.

'Goodnight. Never leave me. I hope the potion you make is a sweet scent to my nostrils.'

'It will be. Sometimes we will be separated but remember I will always be with you in spirit.' Then he spoke aloud, saying, 'Time to sleep,' as he handed Buddy back to Bertie.

As Stentorian hovered down the hallway with Betty, Bertie called to Stentorian, 'Who were you talking to?'

Stentorian stopped and looked at His Lordship. 'I was talking to Rosebud.'

Bertie looked down at Buddy and then looked at M. 'What, she understood?'

Looking, he said, 'Yes, she understood.'

Stentorian began to go on his way, but Bertie called out to him again.

'Stentorian.'

'What?'

'A chip off the old block,' said Bertie.

Both human and creature smiled in their own way.

'What was all that about, when Stentorian held Buddy in the air? I mean, I will ask him, but what did you make of it? Also, one moment Buddy was sobbing and the next she stopped, as soon as Stentorian was near,' said M.

Bertie lay Buddy down in her crib and pulled her silk chrysalis blanket over her. They both looked down at her, smiling at their bundle of joy. Equally, the smiles that were given were given back in the form of the gurgling cooing noises that you would expect from a baby that was very nearly twelve months old.

'Well, I think, I mean, I know this sounds ridiculous but I think Stentorian was talking to Buddy telepathically.'

'No, Bertie, that is impossible.'

Taking M by the hand and looking down at their daughter while she slept, he replied.

'But is it? This is no ordinary baby and we have already seen what power Stentorian has, and Zena. I think they communicated for the first time today and I think Stentorian was just as shocked. Well, not by her being able to communicate telepathically, but by how premature it was.'

They both looked down at their shared bundle of joy. It was hard to believe that such a small human being, well a butterfly being... half human/half insect, had bought so much pleasure to them and everybody at Gladstones Manor.

'Come, let's sleep,' said Bertie.

'Oh yes, but I have some unfinished business with you first!'

'Explain yourself?' said Bertie.

Smirking, Her Ladyship said, 'Oh, I will, but only in private.'

Chapter 6 – Hettie's Domain.

Hettie sat, thinking back to the night Stentorian had arrived at Gladstones Manor… but her memories were not pleasant. After the most shocking night of her life, Hettie was the only one of the staff that remained sceptical about the day's events. Let's face facts. Hettie was very much of the old school. She thought that if the same ideas and principles had worked for her great-grandparents, grandparents and her parents, why should she think or want her life to be any different? Some would think this to be old-fashioned, but it was what she believed in. Life for her had not changed a great deal, for her life was Gladstones. She had never set foot beyond these walls!

She had been born here and she would surely die here and be laid to rest here. So why should she start to believe in these tales of mystery, sorcery and fantasy? Spoof and spooks. Spooks are one thing, but spoofs! Now, she thought, this surely must be one. Yes, there was always a saga to tell, she would agree, but she just could not understand what had unfolded on this day.

Was she ever going to get use to that hideous creature? Gosh, it made the hairs stand up on the back of her neck when she caught a glimpse of him. She would get a shiver down her spine. She would never mean him any harm but he was just gross, vulgar. He was a greyish colour with some sort of moss all over him, she could not quite make out what it was. She had never got close enough and had no intention of doing so. He had a large head that was too big for his body, which was very stocky and thick set, and made his arms appear far too long and slim. It looked like he had no legs, no wonder he hovered everywhere! His hands were so big and his fingers were long and knobbly, which made his hands seem bigger and fingers seem slimmer. But if one thing was true it was that so far he had done nobody any harm here. His eyes were so kind, they didn't seem to fit with the rest of him. Yes, she did have to agree that there was something in his eyes that was kind and inviting. To see him with baby Buddy, yes, even Hettie had to admit the devotion that he had for the baby was something else. Even she had noticed when Buddy was upset and Her Ladyship, Betty and Bertie could not console her, and Stentorian had done the trick, soothing her with ease.

'Is it safe to enter? It's me, Betty! Gosh, something smells good. You have been busy! What a feast!' As she said these words, her mouth started to water and she wondered just how soon she could be eating these delicious goodies! Though she must admit, she would turn her nose up at some of the foods that were on offer!

'Hello there. How are you, Betty? Yes, I have had a busy morning and so I am in for a very quiet afternoon. Please come on in,' she said, smiling. 'This is so exciting!'

'Yes, it is, I cannot wait until tomorrow. I have Stentorian with me.'

The smile was wiped completely from Hettie's face.

'Now, now,' said Betty. 'I am going to make you the best of friends if it is the last thing I do. At least try and get on for tomorrow, please.'

Of course, Stentorian, being Stentorian, was in high spirits most of the time and if he could amuse himself he would. Even if it meant being in the firing line of Hettie's rolling pin and the odd saucepan being hurled through the air in his direction.

'Good morning, your highness,' said Stentorian. On saying these words, Stentorian bowed deeply.

'If you think for one minute, or even a moment, you are going to get around me that way you are very much mistaken. I have work to be getting on with. If you must set up your cauldron then go over there and leave me alone. Just do not mess up my kitchen!'

'Yes, your holiness. But I do not need a cauldron to make my potion. I am not a witch, nor a wizard for that matter. But really, you still think I am the Devil's work, don't you Hettie?'

'I do not know what to make of you; you are certainly not one of us.'

'Well, hooray, we agree on one thing! I am a stone creature and you are a human.'

With that, pop! Stentorian disappeared.

Hettie was not the least impressed with Stentorian's antics and just wished he would disappear into a puff of smoke or go back and vanish into a stone.

'Now where have you gone? Stentorian, where are you?' asked Betty.

Pop! Stentorian's face appeared, making both Betty and Hettie jump out of their skins.

Hettie raised her rolling pin to him.

'I wish you wouldn't do that,' said Betty, raising her eyebrows and smiling at him.

'See you in a minute. I just have to go and speak to Doris about making open sandwiches and other savoury dishes for tomorrow. While I have gone, please do not mess up my kitchen!' As Hettie said these words, she looked straight at Stentorian with a suspicious look. 'I have my eyes on you, Stentorian.'

As soon as Hettie's back was turned Stentorian said, 'I have my eyes on you too, Hettie.' With that, Stentorian made his eyes pop right out of their sockets, which stretched out at least a foot.

'That is disgusting.'

'Oh, she is impossible! I have tried so hard to be her friend. I just have to get a bigger cauldron, spell book and a toad.'

'Stentorian, stop it. You really are upsetting Hettie.'

'Well, she deserves it, thinking I need a cauldron. Whatever next?'

'Stentorian, I will have to conjure up a spell myself and get rid of some of your wit if you don't begin to behave.'

'You would not.'

'I would.'

'Not.'

'Would.'

As they were chanting to one another, they started to chase each other around Hettie's table which was laden with goodies, including little jam tarts, treacle and fruit tarts, queen cakes, jam roly poly, apple pies, rice puddings, rotting fruit, a vast selection of plants that had been potted individually by Horace from the butterfly garden, sugared water which had been prepared and was now being kept at a certain temperature, several plates of dead slugs that had been sun dried (Stentorian's favourite – he found them to be very moreish), Bog bean, which was drunk by Stentorian's family and his kind (to you and me a bitter beer), a plate of slime which looked quite revolting but was actually the staple of Stentorian's diet. It would be quite terrible if one got their wings stuck in this lumpy goo. The goo was a waste product of food! And that was only the puddings and desserts. There was also small pots of pollen which could be sprinkled onto green leaves, which the butterfly beings found to be scrumptious, and bottles of nectar. Gosh, it was one thing arranging food for humans but to make food for other beings as well was a feat in itself. Hettie really had done very well, though everybody had helped, as it had not been easy to organise. Hettie, Doris and other staff that were being hired for the day were making open sandwiches tomorrow.

Hettie would soon be back to pack the food away into the fridge, ready for the very special event the next day, but Betty and Stentorian were having so much fun they didn't realise. They were running and hovering so fast that they knocked one of Hettie's large plate of jam tarts over. They stopped instantly. Oh no, they knew they would be in for it now.

'We are so in trouble,' said Betty, swallowing hard.

Buddy remembered looking back now, Stentorian and Betty were not the only ones in trouble with Hettie where food was concerned. Years later, Glitter and her caused the infamous sick bucket incident. Buddy and Glitter were so sick because they had eaten so much. How we hated ourselves for eating so late at night! They had crept down in the night for a midnight feast, but on eating the last marshmallow and gulping down the last mouthful of fizzy pop they both regretted this. Buddy had eaten far too much food – her body simply could not contain such a huge volume. Laughing out loud, Buddy could remember Glitter and herself squabbling over the last marshmallow, their favourite. Oh, how they wished they had listened to the wise old words of cook, their beloved Hettie. The whines, whimpers and constant groans came shortly after, accompanied by an 'I told you so, do not creep down and sneak into the pantry for goodies,' from Hettie. Smiling to herself, she did not need photographs; all of hers were stored away in her mind maps. What great memories she had.

'Quick, Stentorian, do something. Please be quick, I hear footsteps!'
     As Betty spoke her last word, the kitchen door flung wide open. There, standing in the doorway, was a not-so-happy Hettie.
     'Yes, I am intrigued, I am listening. I leave you for five minutes and bedlam reigns. To think, we have all this space and yet you choose to use up your surplus energy in my kitchen. I heard the crash and I just knew you had knocked one of the plates of food onto the floor,' said Hettie.
     They both looked at Hettie and then at the crushed jam tarts on the floor. They turned to look back at Hettie, their faces full of remorse, but they noticed that they were no longer the focus of Hettie's attention. Hettie tried to lift her foot from the floor,

but found that she could not, no matter how hard she tried, as it was stuck to the floor with jam.

'We are really sorry, we will clean up the mess and...'

'Don't tell me to make another plate of jam tarts to replace the ones that you knocked onto the floor,' said Hettie, with her face now looking somewhat flushed. Betty knew it was time for Stentorian and herself to make a quick exit.

'I will go and fetch a mop and bucket, and then you can clean up the mess you have both made,' Hettie said, using all of her strength to detach herself from the floor and then storming from the room.

'Quick, Stentorian, do something – before Hettie comes back.'

'Do something? What, do what?'

'Oh, Stentorian, you know exactly what I would like you to do!'

Stentorian began to work a little magic, concentrating hard on the mess on the floor. As he stood with his eyes alight and the palms of his hands upright and facing the mess, the tarts were mended and transported back onto the table. Then, he turned his attention to the mess on the floor – one look with his eyes and the mess was gone.

'There we are,' said Stentorian. 'As good as new.'

'Well done, fantastic,' said Betty, squeezing Stentorian's arm. 'Come on, let's go over there and start to make the potion for Buddy.'

'So, what's been going on? Where has the mess gone?' asked Hettie when she returned.

Stentorian and Betty looked at each other.

'Well, yes, we made the mess and so we thought it was only right that we cleaned it up,' said Stentorian.

Hettie looked at him suspiciously, and noticed that the large plate of jam tarts were back on the table and were as good as new.

'How did the plate of jam tarts get back on the table? How did that happen?'

'Hettie, look, we are sorry for the mess we made but as you can see we have sorted it out,' said Betty.

'More like sorcery has sorted the mess than you two,' she said in a whisper as she turned and walked to the parlour to take the mop and bucket back.

'Pardon?' said Betty.

With a raised voice, Hettie said, 'It does not matter.'

Betty and Stentorian were left to make the potion, but not for long, however, as there was soon a knock at the door. The door opened slightly and Doris poked her head into the room.

'Hello, it's only me.'

'Hello, Doris.'

'Hello, busy. What are you doing? Where is Hettie?'

'Hettie's in the parlour, putting the mop and bucket away. We both made a mess and Stentorian sorted it out.'

'Yes, and did not need the mop and bucket.'

Doris looked at Stentorian and he gave her a wink. Doris put her forefinger to her lips, as Hettie returned, anxious to regain control of her kitchen.

'Hettie? Oh, the feast looks delicious, so splendid. I forgot to ask, what time do you need me tomorrow?'

'Well, most of it,' said Hettie, looking down at the sundried slugs and the boiled spiders.

'Well, to be fair, they probably think that our food is not at all palatable either.'

'What time would you like me to come down tomorrow?'

'Well, does Her Ladyship need you at 10am?'

'No, you know Her Ladyship; if you need me at that time she will be happy for me to come.'

'Okay, see you at 10am, I am taking the afternoon off. Bye you two and remember.'

'Oh, before I go, Stentorian, Horace has asked me to ask you if you have enough pollen now.'

Looking up across the table, Stentorian scanned the surface of the table. 'Yes, I think so. I think Zena will pop in later just to check. But yes, thanks Hettie.'

'Oh, I did nothing,' she stammered, and started to blush. She promptly turned and walked out of the room. As the door closed behind her, she called out, 'Thank you, and see you all later.'

For the first time, Stentorian had seen Hettie in a different light. He believed she was starting to warm to him.

'Remember,' called Hettie through the closed door.

'Yes, we know, no mess!'

'So, what goes into a potion? And why spend time making a potion when it would surely be quicker and simpler to work some of your magic, Stentorian.'

'Betty, I keep telling you, magic is not there to be abused and has to be used wisely. It all depends on what part of the body I am trying to heal or cure. Remember, all plants have a purpose and are grown not just to look good, but for their aromatic essences. This is where the plants get their smell, taste, potency and medicinal properties from.'

'So, how do we get the essences from the flowers and plants?'

'Good question. The plants or flowers have to be steamed.'

'Wow, I did not think of a plant giving us so much.'

'Well, in my world we could not live without them. They give us so much. The common winter cress is rich in vitamin C and is used when we have colds.'

'The common winter cress. We eat cress in salads and sandwiches.'

'You would not want to eat this cress raw; it is completely different to the one you eat.'

'So, stone creatures get colds?'

'Yes, believe it, we do. Torment's astringent roots we use for toothache, its flowers are very similar to the buttercup. Feverfew, whose flowers look like daisies, we grow for the drug it contains. It reduces fever and relieves headaches.'

'So, when I next suffer with a headache, I know where to come.'

'The roots of the lesser water-parsnip we use a lot to help with swellings. A poultice is made, kept very hot and moist. It is then applied to the wound and helps with inflammation. Solomon's seal roots are made into a powder and then are used on bruises. Lesser burdock soothes burns and sores, mint soothes a stomach and frankincense clears mucous membranes.'

'Mind blowing, Stentorian. You are a walking, talking medicine cabinet.'

'Well, not really, some of these remedies I have mentioned would have been used by your ancestors.'

'Really?'

'Yes, really, but all these plants must be prepared properly and you have to know what you are doing.'

'There, all finished. I will let the essence cool, I will skim it from the water and then bottle the oil up later. That will help Buddy with her breathing.'

'So Eucalyptus will ease Buddy's breathing?'

'Yes,' Stentorian said, as he inhaled the aromas. 'It smells so good.'

The day was coming to a close and soon it would be time for the celebrations to begin, which would mark two significant events in Buddy's life; her first hatch day and two worlds coming together and being united for the first time. This would be the first and last time that everybody would meet like this.

The guest list was very impressive, from humans to butterfly beings and stone creatures. It had taken a long time to arrange and organize, but finally it was nearly time for the party to begin.

Time had gone so swiftly, had it really been a year since Buddy's hatch date and her arrival at Gladstones? A party, wow a party! A party that would commence at midnight at the end of tomorrow and mark the start of a new dawn… Buddy's tomorrow. A new dawn the day after, daybreak would bring more celebrations and continue until the end of this day.

Chapter 7 – Fit for a Princess in the making.

Bertie, M and Buddy had had a satisfactory slumber and were now prepared and enthusiastic to carry on and organise the festivity.

'Darling, would you like to carry Buddy on your back or your front?'

'Well, I think we should take the buggy. She is getting quite heavy in the baby pouch now.'

'How about if I take the carrier that I put on my shoulders? That way we can get a lot more done, hands free,' said Bertie, as he disappeared into the store cupboard between the nursery and their bedroom.

'Okay,' said M, as she finished dressing Buddy in a beautiful, powder-blue, silk dress, with matching bloomers to hide ones nappy.

'You are a gorgeous, gorgeous baby and we love you so very, very much,' said M, kissing Buddy on the forehead and tickling her. Buddy responded with her arms open and legs kicking with sheer delight, gurgling and laughing to her heart's content. They both were giggling uncontrollably as M had picked her daughter up and was now holding her under her arms and swinging her around in circles.

They did not realise they had an audience, but Bertie had been watching the two of them for a while. How he worshipped the ground that M walked on; he would do anything for this woman. He smiled to himself. She had given him so much. Even though they had not been able to conceive their own child, Bertie would have been happy to live a life just with the woman who circled in front of him. Oh, how he so very much adored her. But they had been lucky that Buddy had come into their lives and he would not have had it any other way. He breathed a gentle sigh and was such a happy, contented man.

'Come on you two, as much as it gives me great pleasure to watch you play and giggle, we have got a busy afternoon ahead of us.' Her Ladyship stopped swinging around and stood smiling at Bertie. Buddy looked too and was totally engaged by her father and his voice, almost waiting for the next command.

'You found the carrier, well done.'

'Yes, darling, it was right at the bottom of the cupboard, with new clothes, toys and various other baby products on top of it. You really must not buy so much. Of course, I do not mind you buying some stuff, M, but remember we do not want to spoil Buddy.'

'I know, but I just could not resist the new season's collection,' said M, kissing Bertie passionately on his lips, making his knees turn to jelly and his heart miss a beat.

'Wow, M. Perhaps we could make our excuses and make a quick retreat, after checking everybody's work in the gardens and giving Buddy to Betty,' said Bertie, putting his arms around M's waist, with Buddy now in the middle of her mummy and daddy.

'Darling Bertie, we must get organised. That reminds me,' M replied, looking at her wristwatch and checking the time with the bedroom wall clock. 'I wonder where Stentorian is, and Betty? They are never late. If anything, they normally wake us up.'

'Is the carrier secure? Let me secure the straps a little more around the waist. There you go, does it feel comfortable?'

'Yes,' said Bertie, as he sat down on the chair. M placed Buddy into the carrier and fastened her in. The three set off to find Stentorian, Betty and the Magnificent Four.

They walked down the stairs and looked at the Magnificent Four, who were so excited to see their master that they nearly exploded with delight.

'There, there, how marvellous it is to be appreciated so,' said Bertie, as he bent down to greet the dogs. As he bent down, Buddy's hands reached for the dogs, ready to grab the first thing she could get hold of.

Bending down, M held out her arms and greeted Horatio, Marmaduke, Theodore and Augustine, who instantly ignored Bertie and bounded to Her Ladyship, nearly knocking her to the floor.

'Hello, you four.' Her face lit up as she saw her four hairy-legged zesty boys. 'Who would like to go out into the gardens and get some fresh air?'

Well, the barks said it all. Off they all went to find out what was happening in the gardens.

There was a hive of activity, with men carry, fetching, erecting, sorting, calling, and hammering, up ladders tying ribbons onto the trees. Lanterns were being hung and lit for when dusk fell and if you were not careful, you would have got completely in the way and caught up in the activities of the afternoon.

'Good afternoon, Horace, and Simpkins. How are the arrangements coming along?'

'Yes, very well, sir, considering we cannot find Stentorian anywhere. We just needed...'

'To ask, check a few details with him,' said Horace.

'I wonder where he is,' said Bertie.

'Has anyone seen Betty?' asked M.

'No,' said Simpkins.

'How very strange,' said M.

'I am sure they will turn up, they're probably up to their usual antics,' said Horace and Simpkins, laughing.

'Okay, well it looks splendid. You have done us both very proud, thank you. M, Buddy and I will walk around the grounds and check the arrangements. We are on the hand-held radios so please contact us if you have any problems. Also, when you see Stentorian and Betty please let us know.'

The grounds were very busy, with a big top being erected in the middle of the lawn ready for the acrobats to perform their latest acts of bravery. On either side of the big top was a carousel, the dodgems, a Punch and Judy Show and clowns.

Stalls were being set up all around the perimeter of the big top – it really was like being at a fairground. There was candy floss, toffee apples, popcorn, a coconut shy, a ducking stool, a bucking bronco (for keen equestrians maybe, or for some blithering idiots to see how long they could hold on for dear life before they let go). A "Guess how many sweets are in the jar" stall, a "Give a rabbit a name" stall, and a "Shoot a can three times in a row to win a goldfish" stall.

There would also be numerous attractions in place happening periodically throughout the festivities: a man on stilts, a man blowing fire, a man juggling, balloons on strings (though there was nobody to hand them out yet), jesters welcoming guests at the gates and keeping beings happy (at whose expense, it would be interesting to see). An ice cream and fish and chip van had been hired, and chefs were on hand to cook up some delicious cuisine. These ten chefs were known for their fabulous barbecues!

Also, food was going to be put out on the dining room table and humans, butterfly beings, stone creatures and beings were able to help themselves. Not all the food would be laid out in one go – this was to keep it fresh and stop the food going off in the heat. As the plates of food emptied, they would be replenished as needed.

There was also a bar stocked with every wine, beer, ale, cider and liqueur imaginable, as well as grand selections of non-alcoholic drinks if anyone wanted to quench their thirst and did not want to have a hangover from hell in the morning. Who wanted to vomit, close their eyes and have the room spin until they had lost consciousness? Then, in the morning, have a headache so bad that even if you wanted to retire and have a snooze in the afternoon, they could not because the constant banging on the inside of one's head reminded them of their mistake? Has that put anyone off drinking yet? No, it has not.

The non-alcoholic bar included: fruit punches, homemade fruit juices, smoothies, milk-shakes, carbonated drinks which some children enjoyed so much, thoroughly loving the high caffeine and sugar content, much to the annoyance of their parents. And why should they not indulge? Where is the harm? Everything in moderation. After all, they do not drink fizzy carbonated drinks all the time, do they? There were water machines also dotted around the grounds.

A cake stall containing all the favourites: Victoria sandwiches, gooey chocolate cakes, carrot cakes, chocolate brownies, flapjacks, fairy cakes, fruit cakes, and coffee and walnut cakes. The varieties were an amazing sight indeed.

A coffee bar and also a char bar (tea) were there. Come on, the grandparents would tire sooner rather than later. They needed to be kept happy, and no one had ever seen a grandparent unhappy with a cup and saucer in their hands? Oh, and a wedge of Victoria sandwich on a side plate waiting to be devoured.

'Well, all that is needed now is to check with Hettie and Doris that all is well.' Looking around, M was pleased with all of the arrangements. It looked wonderful and it was going to be a jolly, splendid time indeed.

'What do you think, Buddy? What do you think about what is unfolding in front of your eyes, mm?' asked Bertie.

Well, there was no answer, as Buddy had fallen asleep with all the excitement. And the party had not even started yet!

'Fast asleep I am afraid, darling. Come on, you four, let's go and see if we can find a stone creature and a nanny,' said M.

They certainly did not have to go far before they came across just who they were looking for. On entering the kitchen, they came upon a sight which would have totally shocked them a year earlier. But things had changed a great deal here at Gladstones and nothing would surely shock them again... or would it?

As they approach the kitchen, Horatio, Marmaduke, Theodore and Augustine promptly looked up at their mistress.

'Good boys, you stay here and wait for my return.' Her Ladyship patted the dogs and gave them all a hug.

'I do not like the sound coming from beyond the kitchen door, M, I just know it is to do with Stentorian and Betty.

'Are you ready? One, two, three.' Bertie opened the door to the kitchen.

Bertie was in shock and M peered over his shoulder tentatively.

'Thank the Lord you came. My arms are killing me,' said Betty.

'Oh, relief! But wait a minute, I do not know how you can help though,' said Stentorian, as he did not know how much more he could take being stuck in this gooey slime.

Bertie and M moved closer to take a better look, wondering why Stentorian and Betty were stuck up to their armpits in this sticky, gooey, gorgy mess.

'Stop, do not come any closer!' warned Betty.

'Well, why not?'

'If we are to help we will have to get close, to see what can be done,' said Bertie.

'It will get you too!' said Stentorian.

'You mean to tell us that whatever is in the cauldron has you rooted to the spot? Am I correct?

'Yes,' said Stentorian.

'Can you not work some magic?' asked M.

'Unfortunately not. As you can see I am completely immersed. I need my hands free to make the magic work.'

'How about if we hold you around the waist and pull you out?'

'The suction is too great. They have a firm hold,' said Stentorian.

'You talk as if the goo is alive,' said M.

'It is,' said Betty.

Bertie and M looked at each other disbelievingly, then back at Stentorian and Betty. Then they heard it talk.

'We've got you this time, he he he.'

'Is it harmful?'

'Yes, when it's exposed to the air it multiplies very quickly. It's weakest when it's in your mouth, though, it cannot handle the moistness.'

'So we need to suffocate it, make it moist as if it were in your mouth,' said Bertie.

'Yes, that's what we need to do, before it becomes too large and we have no hope of controlling it,' said Stentorian. 'Just be careful they do not outwit you before you have time to cover the cauldron.'

'What shall I use?'

'Hettie keeps a pile of muslin over there,' said Betty.

'Oh, we are going to be smothered?' said the goo.

Buddy had been woken up by Stentorian's voice and was smiling at him and talking telepathically with her friend. She asked him what he was doing and said how ridiculous he looked. Up to his armpits in his own food, really, he was not setting a very good example. Stentorian had answered with a knowledgeable look and had said it was easily done when preparing his food. It all happens so, so terribly easy as one day, little Rosebud, you would find out.

'Can you concentrate, Stentorian?' asked Bertie.

'I think Stentorian and Buddy were otherwise engaged.'

'Pardon?'

'In conversation,' explained M.

'Pardon?'

'Darling, does the term telepathy mean anything to you?'

90

'Oh, oh yes, of course, amazing,' Bertie said, trying to look at his talented daughter. Is she doing it now?

'No. Please, sir, can you please bring the muslin? Look, they are multiplying even more. But wait, take the backpack off your back and give Buddy to Her Ladyship. Buddy is too young to come into contact with these goo creatures.'

'Oh dear, they are the most disgusting thing I have ever seen,' Betty said, looking down into the gooey mess. 'It's got a head, trunk and limbs, gross.' She squeezed her eyes shut, to save herself from the torment.

Bertie sat on a chair while M unstrapped Buddy from the backpack. With the empty backpack still strapped on Bertie's back, he grabbed the muslin and put it over the cauldron.

'What is that climbing down the side of the cauldron, Bertie?'

'It's one of them escaping. Quick, grab it and throw it back in the pot,' said Stentorian.

'Yes, I can see into it. It looks very sweet in its own way.'

Opening one eye, Betty said to Her Ladyship, 'You cannot be serious.'

Bertie pulled the slippery, slimy creature from the side of the cauldron, which was difficult as it had padded feet which acted as suckers, enabling it to stick to almost anything it put its mind to.

'Yes, I agree. It's quite sweet in its own little way. Smooth little body with a personality all of its own.'

'Don't be fooled, it is not as sweet as you think. Put it back in the pot, sir, please.'

'Oh, it seems a shame.'

'Sir, please.' Stentorian was now pleading with him.

As soon as Bertie had decided to put the gooey monster back, it turned and gave Bertie a frightful nip on his finger.

'Ouch!' And with the pain of the beastly nip, he picked up a corner of muslin that was draped over the cauldron and flung the little monster in. Ignoring the cries of 'oh no, please, not in the pot,' coming from this slimy form, Bertie quickly put the corner of the muslin back and held his hand on top. Bertie, who was not a violent man, picked up his right hand and now was surveying the damage to it. It was bleeding profusely and he was annoyed that he had been fooled. Clenching his fist and banging the lump beneath the muslin flat, he yelled, 'My hand is so sore!'

'Never mind, we can sort them. Well done,' said Stentorian.

'Now, what's happening? The slime suddenly feels less sticky. Is it working, Stentorian?'

'Yes. Quick, sir. Grab me by the waist and pull hard. See if you can pull me free.'

With his hand in pain, Bertie pulled with all his worth, and with a squelchy, squishy noise, Stentorian was free to work his magic and return the contents of the cauldron to a safe, juicy consistency. The concoction was now safe but a valuable lesson had been learnt today: what happens if the ingredients of this recipe become too sticky and solid. Watch out, little monsters will start popping out of your food!

'Betty, are you all right?' everybody asked, crowding around her.

'Yes, I think so,' she said, looking down at her arms, which felt so sore after being in the same position for so long.

'Hooray, hooray!' The party was a rip-roaring success... the years rolled by and Gladstones was magnificently impressive in every way. Everybody was so happy, and of course, Buddy, the little one, enchanted everyone she met. This sometimes shocked her parents but as she grew, she had the power to inspire devotion and was full of enthusiasm in everything she learnt.

Beings soon became aware that all was not as it seemed. Every stone had been turned, or so it seemed. Had one ugly stone not been turned? Was this going to be the beginning of the end of Gladstones? Or the end of the beginning?

Stentorian was the teacher, the great pedagogue. Her Ladyship wished he would not be so strict when teaching Bud. In time, she learnt that she had to sit tight and sit back, letting Stentorian take control.

And take control he did. Stentorian insisted on a strict observance of rules and regulations, though this was only to protect Bud from herself and from her worlds, Gladstones and Greenlands.

Before long, The Elders came to Gladstones, to observe Stentorian teaching their next heir to the throne.

'Remember, your kind are frivolous but you will have to be serious at all times, even as a child,' said my mentor.

'But, how do I do this?' I questioned.

'Always remember… "You will find a way, no matter how hard the path you tread." A problem is as small or as big as you would like it to be. There is always an answer to a question. There is always a solution to an unsolved puzzle. No matter how bad an outcome, the puzzle has to be completed. And lastly, Bud, no matter how many lies are told, the truth will out', he said. 'Now, that's the end of our classes for today. And tomorrow we will learn more in order to…?'

'I learn and keep learning all about my worlds in order to survive and save another day,' I said, repeating the mantra as I had done every day since our lessons began.

Chapter 8 – The Butterfly Doctor.

The years had rolled past so quickly it seemed as if they had wings attached to them. I was now ten but my mind was going on twenty! It was time, time for me to know all there was to know about myself and my species. It was tough, sometimes, being me. Gosh, I hated the legacy that had been bequeathed to me. At times, I stamped my foot in total protest of simply being me. At times, the arguments and raised voices were simply too much to bear. What was to be expected was at times simply too much to comprehend. I did act up somewhat and acted like a little diva, but it was only sometimes and I was only ten at the time. Being ten is tough at the best of times but knowing your destiny was even tougher still.

It was beyond anything I could comprehend. I fought against the reality of the situation; three worlds were colliding and I was supposedly going to stop this from happening. I was going to be everyone's saviour – me! I could not imagine how I was going to do this. Can you imagine for just a second what that felt like? So, being a little bit of a diva was just my way of saying "enough" to all the adults and species of my worlds.

I just wanted to have a normal childhood, to do what other ten-year-olds did – meeting with friends in the neighbourhood, playing knock down ginger, being in nature, going out exploring all day long, on rainy days playing with marbles or dolls. Dolls weren't really my thing, apart from my favourite doll called Lucy. Nan had knitted her a blue woollen overcoat, matching long johns with an elasticated waist. A beautiful woollen blouse, with puffed sleeves, was worn under the overcoat. My Nan was partially sighted, but that didn't stop her from being a fantastic knitter. Sad to say I could never knit anything but a perfect square. I laugh now at the memory of learning plain and purl knitting, "knit one drop one stitch." I always said to Nan, "But I have a hole two lines down," and she would say "Then you dropped too many stitches." Those days were fun, when I could really forget who I was and my namesake for just a while. Board games were a favourite, but there simply was not the time to play. Lady M taught me French knitting but I got bored easily as all I was ever left with was a long piece of knitted wool that had its end out of an old cotton reel with four little tack nails placed in a square on top of the cotton reel. On each nail you were supposed to attach a loop of wool and work from there, but I always ended up with the reel looking like it had given birth to a long knitted worm and I was left wondering what the purpose of this was.

Stentorian also knew that the strain was too much and allowed me to be a child some days, at the protest of my elders. They would frown terribly at a little ten-year-old girl and expected lesson after lesson, all about me and my worlds. Even though I seemed like a diva, in my mind I simply wanted to be a child. Besides, everyone knew who the true little stamp-footed diva was at Gladstones. Yes, it was my beloved Glitter, my beautiful unicorn.

'Are you sure about that?' asked Stentorian with a wink in his eye, reading my mind again.

'Yes, quite sure, thank you,' I said.

Gosh, what a two-way communication we had! We would often bounce ideas around our two heads, with no need for talking. We never had any secrets, which could be very annoying. Stentorian always heard my thoughts as he was telepathic, but it was a way of protecting me.

Why, oh, why did I have to learn all this paraphernalia "in order to survive and save another day"? Gosh, I woke up hearing this phrase and fell asleep hearing this phrase, literally ringing in my ears like a constant gong… oh, how I wished I had been born into a world of nothingness.

So here we were, Stentorian, Glitter and I, ready for yet another quest. But this time was different, it was finally for me to be introduced to the Butterfly Doctor. I had heard so many stories about this allusive Butterfly Doctor. I had heard he was the stuff of mere legend, nobody had ever really met him. Supposedly, the Butterfly Doctor was far too busy to see his patients, so he would send one of his assistants to attend to the sick, frail and the infirm. I started to wonder if he really existed at all, thinking the stories I heard were merely myths but now I realised he was not a myth at all and very much alive, well and flitting.

'So what is he really like, Stentorian?' I said, forever inquisitive.

'What makes you think that the doctor is a he? Why presume the gender?' asked Stentorian.

'Well, I presumed,' I said.

'Buddy, to presume something is what it might seem could and most certainly will get you into a predicament that you may not be able to get yourself out of,' said the forever wise Stentorian.

I started to roll my eyes and then he said, 'In a moment you are going to bend your antenna and then where will you be?' We both stared and I started laughing.

'Oh, can I never be left alone with my own thoughts and ideas? Why, oh, why do you have to share all of those too?' I asked.

'I am afraid that is the way I am. You just need to accept for now that I am in your thoughts. When you have reached all your milestones and fought many battles, then, and only then, can I leave you alone with your thoughts,' said Stentorian.

'Gosh, Stentorian, you are like a walking talking encyclopaedia,' I muttered under my breath. I just wished he could give me my thoughts back and just let me explore them on my own.

'I heard that, but I will take it all on board and accept it as a compliment…' said the stone creature.

I was now fuming, I felt as if I was going to blow a gasket. He stared intensely at me and I did the same in return, learning from this great teacher. 'Oh I know, but why do you have an answer for everything I say?' At this point, I could consciously feel the heat radiating from my body, and see the sweat beads forming on my nose. Stony, stony, short, hairy, organised dwarf – no, midget.

'Because I do, Buddy. Someone has to in order to ensure your survival,' said the stone creature.

'I heard that too, but yes, stony I am. Remember, sticks and stones,' he said.

'Yes,' I said, 'and names will never hurt me. Nor will the dead, only beings walking and talking have the ability to hurt with their verbal speech or expressions.'

'Sometimes the dead will haunt us for sure, but I will leave that lesson for another day. At the moment we have enough to discuss,' he said.

'Oh, for goodness sake,' I said, my voice raising.

With this I stomped into my room and sat down on my chair, feeling the steam emerging from my body. I was totally feeling sorry for my hatch right (the human equivalent of a birth right). He instantly came hovering in the doorway.

'Look, remember your place. Respect your elders and remember that as you grow every conversation we have will become clearer. There is a reason for the topics we discuss which will become clear over time, you will see. Please control your feistiness, you may lose too much of your body heat, which would be dangerous for you,' said an oh-so-calm Stentorian.

'Words do not have to always be spoken, do they?' I asked Stentorian.

'No, sometimes no words are needed to explain how we feel. Emotions are the most powerful tools we are given, as long as they are used correctly and we use them to gain knowledge of how to become a bigger, better being. Thoughts and ideas are just fine too, to feel is just fine too.' With that, Stentorian gave me something similar to what humans do... that huggy thing.

'Thank you,' I said.

'Bud, remember, a word is just a word, but sometimes actions speak louder,' he said, and I finished his sentence.

'Louder than words.' Smiling at my mentor, I knew I had learnt so much, but still had an awfully long way to go and a lot more knowledge to absorb.

'Yes, you do,' said Stentorian.

I was only ten (very soon to be eleven) and sometimes I simply could not take all this knowledge on board. It was immense pressure, and the more I seemed to fight it the harder my life became. The days when I accepted my hatch right the lessons became so much easier. I knew all of this, so why was I making my life harder then what it needed to be?

'Exactly,' said Stentorian.

I began drifting in and out of my own thoughts, to a place of nothingness. I guessed this was a form of escapism for me.

'If it helps, do it,' said Stentorian.

'What, play with my thoughts?' I asked, bemused.

'Yes, play with your thoughts,' said Stentorian.

It will not change anything, even if I play with them, throwing my ideas of life into the air. It will not change the way I feel. It will make no difference, I thought. It will not make me who I would like to be.

'Yes, but maybe imagine Glitter in your place,' said Stentorian.

I promptly laughed out loudly and replied, 'How on earth could Glitter sort out three worlds and the collision? I will one day be known as Queen Buddy, or, I am guessing, Zena the second.'

'Now, there is a title to live up to,' said Glitter.

'Yes, but it is what you make it,' said Stentorian.

'How?' I asked, bewildered.

'Just think of it as a name change,' suggested Stentorian.

'A name tag,' said Glitter.

It was at that moment that Glitter walked up to me snuffled his wet muzzle under my chin.

'Come on, Bud. You are you, I am me and that is that. Shall I do my impression of what a half-horse, half-butterfly would look like?' suggested Glitter.

Smiling, I looked up at my best buddy in the whole wide world and simply said, 'No, because it was messy last time and we rolled around so much I crushed my scales!'

'So,' said Stentorian, 'Are we ready to appear, hover, flit or pop?'

Glitter and I both looked at each other, faces expressionless, stunned.

It was a terrible journey from Gladstones to Greenlands as the map told, which was etched on my secret wall inside the great hall where nobody could see it or make out what it was really about. The journey was extremely dangerous, with perils and pitfalls never very far away. The quest was only made when only completely necessary.

Stentorian was ready, with his walking stick in one hand and his other hand free to see the way.

I had packed Glitter's saddle bag to the brim and nothing else would have fitted. Not even his hairpin for his hair at bedtime.

'Buddy, if you put that on my back I will resemble some sort of pack horse, a mule ready for its climb into the Himalayas.'

'You know, I swear you should have been a mare. For a talking unicorn you're so in touch with your feminine side. But, gosh, I do adore you so much, Glitter.' With that I put my arms around his neck, choking him half to death, because if I could I would smother him with love.

'Buddy, steady with those hugs. You are getting so strong, you must learn to control your embrace, as you could crush Glitter to death. I know you worship him but let him breathe,' said Stentorian, who was getting a little bit concerned about the quest in hand.

'Yes, Buddy, let me breathe!' said Glitter, who was such a drama queen he started coughing on purpose, pretending he was dying. 'When we get to the doctor, I need a prescription.'

I was now laughing. 'There is nothing wrong with you! Gosh, you are such a hypochondriac,' I said, smirking.

'Would you two stop with your frolicking? Bud, on a serious note, take heed and listen. You could easily choke Glitter to death, stop with the strong embraces. Now, can I ask, are we appearing, flying or walking?' said Stentorian.

But I was too stunned by his first statement to even consider his question. 'Could I really send Glitter to pass?' I asked.

Yes, but if you listen and learn to control your inner strength you will be fine. This is why we are visiting the doctor. He needs to tell you all about yourself and how you can learn to control your inner strength,' said Stentorian.

Glitter and I shared a look, then turned back to Stentorian with wide-eyed expressions and frowns that left furrows so deep on our foreheads it looked like we had reached old age prematurely.

'So, what is the quest to be?' he asked.

'Appearing,' we both eagerly said together.

'Appearing it is then,' declared Stentorian.

'Yippee,' Glitter and I said, jumping up in the air together.
So off we went to the Butterfly Garden to the place where the buddleia tree stood. This was the point where Stentorian could see the way home, the way back to the old market square, where the grasses were forever green, where seasons never changed and the sun always shone... Greenlands.

We appeared in Greenlands as if we had never ever left. It was a great feeling to feel right back at home where I belonged. It was more or less instant, from one world to another, when we travelled this way and it was the safest way to travel if the seasons were in harmony with one another and my three worlds, which were ever closer to colliding.

Stentorian and I held hands while each of us held a hoof from Glitter fronts legs. Glitter stood on his hind legs, wearing a wrap rug to protect his modesty.

'Can we hurry up with this part? My bits are going to shrivel if I stay in this position for much longer,' said a red-faced Glitter. Gosh, he was so bashful.

We arrived a little before high hours, which in Greenlands meant time was getting late. As we arrived, I noticed the air was gripped with an icy cold chill. But Greenlands was always warm... This should not be.

'I am glad we did not fly. Your wings, Bud, would have iced over or, even worse, split or broke in the icy cold air,' said a worried looking stone creature.

'Not good,' said a frowning unicorn.

'Oh,' I said. 'But what would have happened if I was flying?'

'You know all about gravity,' said Glitter.

'Glitter,' warned Stentorian, with a raised eyebrow.

'Bud has to know the consequences of all that we do' said a comforting Glitter.

'What would have happened to me?' I asked, getting frustrated.

'My darling Bud, you would have fallen to earth with a sudden thud... and crumbled into many pieces,' said a grim looking Glitter.

The colour drained from my complexion, I felt my skin go all clammy and even my insides felt pale. I needed to sit down, but before I could instead I fell to the ground with a thud.

'Oh no, Buddy is going into shock!' declared Stentorian.

101

'Oh no, oh no, not good, not good at all... oh no, not good,' said a near-hysterical Glitter, running around in circles.

'Bud,' said Stentorian.

'Bud,' said Glitter, pushing his muzzle into me, 'Get up get up.'

'No good, we need the Butterfly Doctor,' said a frightened Stentorian.

'Our quest must begin. We need him more than ever to appear,' said Stentorian. 'But Glitter, try not to worry. This is a forever shifting change, with the climates and the worlds coming closer. Bud has picked up on this and her bodies cannot seem to cope.'

Looking down onto the situation, gosh, I did look somewhat ill and it was amazing how the colour had simply drained from me I had become a shell of my former self. Stentorian picked me up from the ground and cradled me in his arms, with Glitter blowing warm air onto me to give me an instant blanket of warmth.

I simply resembled a rag doll.

'No need,' I said, opening my eyes. 'I am fine.' I tried to get up out of Stentorian's arms.

'Careful,' said Stentorian and Glitter together.

'Buddy, sit on Glitter and I will lead him,' said Stentorian.

So, we arrived into Greenlands, into the old market square, where we headed straight for the Butterfly Doctor's house, which was situated just off of the main square up some steep, old, stony steps which were actually built into the side of the house. The staircase seemed never-ending – I was certain Glitter was going to give Stentorian and I earache by complaining the whole way. Oh, he was a complainer, but we adored him to pieces. Gosh, we did get earache; my slits ached for an entire week. Stentorian was fine, as he would hover to the top.

Once at the top, we came to a rickety, old wooden door that complemented the exterior walls of the building. Stentorian was neither big enough nor tall enough to reach, and I was not allowed to even try, just in case I harmed my hands, so it was Glitter who bent his head down and pressed the buzzer with his horn. If we had known the buzzer was going to be like a siren, shaking the entire building, and the rest of the town, we would have climbed in through the window.

'Oh, my lord, if His Lordship had heard this he would have gone completely bonkers and ripped it off the wall!'

'It is like the gong for dinner! What a stupid noise,' said Glitter.

'Here, here. It really is hurting my slits,' I said, with my hands on my slits.

'Buddy, sit still in your saddle and close your eyes,' said Stentorian.

Eventually, the noise stopped and the door came open. It opened surprisingly quickly for such a heavy, thick door, making us all jump. We looked at one another, and in we went. Of course, at the time I was unaware that I had a gift, but would find this out much later on.

It was dark, dank and dreary in the house and as I rubbed my eyes I was glad to say they were totally able to cope and adjust to the dim light that presented itself before us. The only light in the room was from a candle which flickered in the far corner. Somewhere there must have been a draught seeping in, as otherwise why would the candle be flickering? The candle stood on a desk that could barely be seen under all the paper and files that were heaped up in piles on top. Behind the desk was a chair, and in the chair was a dark, hunched silhouette of a being. The light cast shadows on the wall and I saw the same things that I had growing and sprouting from my head, but on a massive scale, the likes of which I had never seen before. Was he a giant of my species?

'Antennas,' I said with excitement as I jumped down from Glitter and walked confidently towards the crumpled figure in the corner. 'You have them too, I—'

'I do indeed... Who am I?' asked the Butterfly Doctor.

'You must be the elusive Butterfly Doctor.' I said, as I appeared at the front of the desk, looking up at him. I had to stand on tip toe to look over all the paperwork on his desk, as he in turn stared down at me over his glasses.

'Do you read my thoughts too?' I asked.

'Yes, but a little differently from Stentorian, who I believe reads them all the time,' said the Butterfly Doctor. 'It is time to tell you a little about yourself. I have prepared diagrams so as to show you your anatomy. If you will all be seated on the chairs provided, the lesson can begin.'

There were three little, wooden chairs, that were waiting for us to sit upon them. In front of them was a blackboard and a little shelf, running from one end to the other, with a container of chalks and a big rubber to clear the unwanted lesson from the day before. So we were all seated.

'Buddy, you are a unique specimen,' he said.

'You make me sound as if I should belong in a jar,' I said.

'No, not at all,' said the doctor. 'Please, let me explain. You are a butterfly being, you are neither human nor a butterfly.'

'Am I not just me?'

'Yes, but a species that has been existing for millions of years living beside humans. Your species knows it but the humans do not.'

'Buddy, you have two skeletons, as you are both a human and a butterfly.'

'Now I am totally confused,' said Buddy.

'Well, do not fear, this is why I bought you here,' said Stentorian.

Butterflies have skeletons, just like humans, but their skeletons are on the outside of their bodies, and are called exoskeletons. This protects the insect (you), and keeps water within your body so you do not dry out. '

'But wait a minute – she has two,' said Glitter.

'Yes, two, as humans have one as well,' said Stentorian.

'Yes, this is correct. Humans have skeletons to protect their major organs and muscles,' said the Butterfly Doctor.

'Wait a minute, so I am a butterfly that has wings, antennae, and feet?'

'Yes, but as you mature, you and all of us will have to be careful not to touch you and your wings,' he said.

There was a sombre feeling in the air. I looked at Stentorian and Glitter then back to the Butterfly Doctor, who all seemed to have the same expression.

I remember screwing up my eyes. 'So, what are you all hiding from me now?' I asked.

'Tell her, just tell her,' said Stentorian.

'Tell me what, what?' I said, alarmed at what I now may hear.

'Your wings. You will sprout a beautiful pair of wings as you go through your change and mature.'

'Change?' I repeated.

'It is called puberty in humans,' said Stentorian.

'Yes, but you will go through both human and butterfly puberty, and we do not yet know how your body will cope with such a dramatic change,' said the Butterfly Doctor.

'Tell me, please,' I insisted, even though I was unsure of what I may hear.

'If you are touched, as a butterfly it will hamper your ability to fly. Your wings work in harmony together, moving as one, like a symphony. The layers are so thin that by touching them you can cause too many layers to come off. Wings are made up of four layers of scales which give them their magnificent colour. Removing the scales can weaken the wing and make it impossible to fly. If you are touched, dust will come off, damaging your wings.'

'Oh,' I said.

'Startling a butterfly by touching it can cause it to go into shock, which in turn can cause… death,' said Stentorian.

'I am not really understanding,' I said, bemused.

Again the room went oh-so-terribly quiet and I knew by everyone's expressions that it was a serious matter.

'Bud, this is not an easy thing to say but it is time. You need to know that… that… that… ' Stentorian simply could not get his words out.

'That…?' I said

'Bud, you could end up killing yourself,' said Glitter, who was, as always, so direct. He was surely American; they were always up front and said what was on their minds.

'Kill myself… but how can I kill myself?'

'You are a human too, which means that oil is seeping from every pore within your body. This oil will weigh you down. You could possibly suffocate yourself from within,' said a straight-faced Butterfly Doctor.

'How can this be? I am not the only one of my kind,' I said.

'No, but for some unknown reason you were born this way. Call it a fluke with the genes, who knows, but this is a serious dilemma that we will have to cope with,' said the Butterfly Doctor.

'Wait a minute, half-human half-butterfly, like Zena?' I said.

'No, no, Zena is a pure butterfly being,' said the Butterfly Doctor.

'But I look like her,' I said.

'Yes, you do, but you are unique. We have had to cope with that since you were an infant,' said Stentorian.

'So, it has been going on for a while?' I said.

'Yes,' said Stentorian and the Butterfly Doctor, with a nod from Glitter.

'Your wings are so very delicate,' said the Butterfly Doctor.

'As thin as the thinnest piece of paper I ever did see,' said Glitter.

'They can be torn so very easily, which is why no one must touch you, no matter how tempting,' said the Butterfly Doctor.

'In love too... we are not sure if you will or ever can be loved,' said Stentorian.

'Love?' I said, confused.

'Yes, love. Because of your complicated anatomy, we are not sure how it will work,' said the Butterfly Doctor, 'Meeting a being and reproducing.'

'Is it not a little too early to be thinking of this? I mean, Bud might not want a partner in crime,' said Stentorian.

'Or babies, for that matter,' I piped up.

'Yes, but is it crucial that Buddy knows the limitations of her body,' said the Butterfly Doctor.

I sat there in shock, pondering what my future would now be...

'Well, for now, we need to teach Buddy the facts about her butterfly body and her human one,' said Stentorian.

And so the Butterfly Doctor began. 'Your body as a butterfly is divided into three regions: the head, thorax—'

'Thorax?' I said.

'Yes, and abdomen, which humans have too,' said the Butterfly Doctor.

'Oh, great, so she has something to be grateful for,' said a disgruntled Glitter.

'Love you too, Glitter,' I said.

'In adults butterflies there are two compound eyes. Each eye is made up of facets. Also, butterflies can see into the ultraviolet range of the light spectrum,' he said.

'That would explain a lot,' said Stentorian.

'Yes of course,' I said.

'Yes, I know what you are both thinking,' said the Butterfly Doctor.

'Well, I do not, so can someone explain?' huffed Glitter.

'Okay, I will explain to you,' I said. 'I can see colour that you cannot. My colour vision extends into ultraviolet.'

'Really?' said Glitter.

'Yes. I see ultraviolet patterns which guide me deeper into flower heads. I use my colour vision when searching for food,' I said.

'So, being sensitive to UV, violet, blue, green and red wavelength's peaks suggests to me colour constancy,' said Stentorian.

'Yes, this is correct,' I said. 'I like to bathe in the direct sunlight, but I like shaded areas too, and to go out on cloudy days. But it is forbidden to go to shady places ever, isn't it?'

'Yes, totally forbidden,' said a forlorn Stentorian.

'Bud, that is an amazing insight about the colours you see,' said Glitter.

'So, the things growing out of your head, Buddy, are called antenna,' said the Butterfly Doctor.

'What, my aerials?' I said, laughing at my own joke.

'We always get a good reception wherever we are,' said Glitter, joining in.

'Well, I'll tell you a little more about this. You may laugh, but you have a built-in navigational system in there,' said the Butterfly Doctor.

Glitter and I looked at each other in confusion.

'What, like a mind map?' asked Glitter.

'Not exactly,' said Stentorian.

'It is a sensory organ that can be used for taste, smell, feel and, yes, to tell you where you are and where to go should you get lost.'

'Wow,' I said, excited. Unfortunately I was most definitely too excited, as I leant forward in joy and bumped my head on the floor, because I simply forgot to save myself. I passed out.

On awakening, I had a hovering Stentorian and a Butterfly Doctor looking over me, with Glitter's eye peering in a gap.

The Doctor scooped me up in his arms, being very careful not to touch my back.

'What happened?' I asked.

'With the excitement you bumped your head and passed out,' said Glitter.

'You never did answer my question about whether or not you can read my thoughts,' I said.

'Yes, I did. I can, but only when you are inside these four walls,' said the Butterfly Doctor. With that, he placed me on his couch and collected a cold compress to cool my clammy head.

'Bud will be all right, won't she?' asked Stentorian nervously.

'She will be fine, as long as she learns about her forever changing anatomy and how to learn to deal with the dangers. If not, it could cause an untimely end, and could most certainly end in paralysis, like her bump just now,' said the Butterfly Doctor.

'Paralysis, just as I thought,' said Stentorian.

'Oh my, oh my dear lord,' said Glitter, holding his left hoof to his forehead and falling against the sofa.

'Now, come on, Glitter, it really is not that bad.'

'Really?' I said as I lifted off the cold compress from my forehead. 'Paralysis sounds pretty much lethal, like the end to me.'

'Oh my... oh dear... oh my...' and that was the last we heard of Glitter for a while, as he fainted and went into a deep sleep.

I started to clamber off of the couch, but was stopped by Stentorian. 'Oh no you don't. Bud, think better of it. Bud, you need to rest.'

'But Glitter needs me.'

I looked imploringly at the Butterfly Doctor, who replied, 'No, you are staying exactly there. Stentorian is right, you need rest and until you learn how to deal with your body we will simply have to wrap you in cotton wool,' said the bossy physician.

'Bossy, hey, well I would rather be bossy then you lose your life,' said a straight-faced Butterfly Doctor.

'But, what is so special about me?' I asked, a little bewildered and tearful.

'All right, this is why we are here,' said Stentorian.

'It is time for you to understand who you are.'

'I am Bud and I am a girl who will one day…'

'Let's stop there. There is not going to be a one day if you continue on your path,' said the Butterfly Doctor. 'You are a special being with so much going on that your body, mind, and soul are having trouble adjusting to. You are half-human half-butterfly with two skeletons and three hearts which cannot keep up with the demands of two skeletons.'

'I think we need to get Bud back to Gladstones. But what about the change, how will Bud know, how will we know?' asked Stentorian.

'Oh, the change is like no other, the metamorphosis is a process of transformation where Bud will not only change in her body but her mind and soul,' said the Butterfly Doctor.

'What are the signs?' I asked.

'You will have a ravenous hunger, a feeling of weakness and a lack of fuel. When you want to eat everything in your path and the beast within takes over, that is when you will know the change is upon you,' he said.

As we walked out, the Butterfly Doctor stopped Stentorian and said, 'Be under no illusions about what you are all dealing with here. Bud will become a stranger to herself, transforming into someone else entirely. Beware of the beast within her. The demons are amongst us.'

Chapter 9 – The Change.

I had been so hungry for days now, eating everything in my path. It was incredible how much I was putting away. It was not just one muffin for afternoon tea and one cucumber sandwich, but three large, American-sized muffins and a full plate of cucumber sandwiches. If I was having afternoon tea with the family, and anybody left half a sandwich or crumbs, I would finish that too.

But one afternoon I gave myself a shock when the family and I were sitting having afternoon tea in the drawing room. I sat, nearly stuffed, but still feeling the need to eat. So, not content with what I had already consumed, I scanned the room for more food. I could smell something. I scanned the room with my eyes and smiled. There, just peeking out from Bertie's newspaper, was a half-eaten smoked salmon and cream cheese sandwich. A fly began buzzing around the room and I knew instantly where it was heading. Suddenly, without me even noticing, my proboscis popped out, uncoiling itself. Who would get there first, me or the fly? But the once fresh sandwiches had already started to develop crusty curled corners. I was not interested in the sandwich – it was the bluebottle that was making my mouth water. I was thinking now about how I wanted to hold the fly within my left thumb and index finger and, using my right thumb and index finger like human pincers, I wanted to pluck its legs from its torso, one by one, and savour this chewy, hairy delicacy. I had never ever experienced this before – my proboscis was so very long and, wow, it acted like a straw. Its appearance shocked not only me but everyone else too – I had just consumed a large bluebottle fly while sitting in the drawing room for afternoon tea , and it had not gone unnoticed.

'What in the world was that, Buddy?' asked Bertie.

Looking sheepishly at my father, I turned and said, 'I am not sure what just happened.'

'Why are you so ravenously hungry, darling?' enquired M.

Looking to my right with the same expression, I said to her, 'I am not sure about that either.'

Stentorian was sitting and Glitter was standing by my side and had seen it also, but they had seen this thousands of times before and to us it was normal practice.

'It was her proboscis,' said Stentorian.

'Ah,' said Bertie.

I giggled at this remark and jumped up and kissed my father on the forehead, saying, 'Father, for such a studious soul sometimes the practically of your brain does not work.'

'We do remember in all of this what we all are dealing with,' said Glitter.

'Buddy is not normal, is she?' remarked M.

'Oh, thank you for that,' I said, smiling, abnormal to my world and my species. I stood up and kissed her gently on the forehead.

She leant into my kiss and had a realisation. 'What is normal? None of us are, and besides, I should hate to be boring and have somebody call this family normal.'

'Yes, dysfunctional I have learnt to live with,' said Bertie.

'I do not think we are dysfunctional at all. Bud is what she is,' said Stentorian.

'I was hatched that way,' I said.

'But the fly… ' Glitter said in disgust.

Over time, my appetite just kept growing and growing. I would never eat just two biscuits, but a whole packet of them. I was devouring over one litre of Coca Cola in one sitting and had hidden empty bottles, packets and containers under my bed in disgrace.

I was stuffing myself silly, growing plumper each day… What was happening to me? As I was pondering this one day, I was standing in the kitchen, reaching for a large packet of crisps. And yes, I was going to eat all twenty individual packs myself.

'It is the change,' said Stentorian.

'The change it is,' said Glitter.

'The change,' I said.

'Yes, the change,' said Stentorian and Glitter together.

'The change,' said Her Ladyship.

'What?' asked Bertie, perplexed.

Her Ladyship leaned into Bertie's ear and must have whispered the puberty human thingy, as father had gone a little pink.

'Right you are. I need to take some air,' he said. With that, he jumped up, kissed me on the forehead and asked Stentorian, 'Do you have everything under control?'

'Control. Well, I would not put it quite like that,' said Stentorian.

At this point I had already consumed three packets of crisps but it felt vital to eat like this, even though I was eating so rapidly that I just could not get the food in my mouth quick enough.

'Well, it is disgusting. I have food around my mouth at the table. My manners have gone completely out of the window,' I despaired.

'It is not your fault, Bud,' said Glitter.

'We will just have to ride this out, though I am concerned at the amount of food you are consuming and the frivolous way you are devouring it. Like a lion at its kill, your eyes look from left to right, watching, guarding, making sure no one will take what rightfully is yours,' said Stentorian.

'I know, it's like I would kill for my food, but I know no one will take it,' I said.

Glitter got up. "Okay, would you like a flake or a ripple?'

Smiling at him, I said, 'What, you have to ask... I will take both.'

'Ha ha ha, or I can fit a mouth bag to your muzzle and we can talk while you munch,' said my lovable unicorn.

'I love your wit and you make me smile, so I will let you get away with that remark,' I said. He was the coolest, funniest unicorn I ever did meet.

Two munches later, the chocolate bars were gone.

Stentorian looked on, worried. "Bud, do you think you are able to slow down on the calorie intake?' he asked.

'I don't know. I feel like I am living in a body of a creature that has completely taken over,' I said.

'Can you explain a little more?' asked Stentorian and Glitter together.

'Well, I am completely different from what I use to be. I feel different from what I was, I am cold one moment and hot the next,' I said.

'These are apparently called the hot sweats,' said Glitter.

'I feel my body racing, as if I am being forced along a racing track at a hundred miles an hour. My body pulses, muscles are pounding and my heart rate races, taking my body to the edge. My skin feels prickly, itchy and dry. I know now I am experiencing the change. I feel powerful and yet strange. I feel my body's blood running away with itself and on standing I fall, as I cannot control the natural force of the racing blood. Racing inside like the beast, I feel as if I have the ultimate power to rule the worlds, but at the same time I cannot seem to steady the flow and control myself. It is too powerful, I am unable to harness the power and turn it into strength. All I can seem to think about is food, food and more food,' I said, the words rushing to leave my mouth.

'Wow,' said Glitter. 'Amazing. It is definitely the change.'

'Do you feel tired?' asked Stentorian.

'Yes, after eating most definitely, after gorging myself on fruit, especially rotting fruit,' I said.

'That is disgusting,' said Glitter.

'Yes I know,' I said, 'but it seems to settle me a little more.'

'The sugars are what you need as you are consuming, your body needs them for the change as so many calories as your cells are being broken down and rebuilding another you,' said Stentorian.

Dusk was upon us and I was feeling so tired. I could feel my eyes begging to be closed.

'Come, let's get ourselves an early night and see what tomorrow brings,' said Stentorian.

'What tomorrow brings. Hmm, I do not know if I like the sound of tomorrow,' said Glitter.

'Me neither,' I said.

'Well, you may have changed then,' said Stentorian.

'Changed?' said Glitter and I together.

'Yes,' said Stentorian.

'What exactly will I be changing into?' I said.

'A butterfly,' said Glitter, laughing.

I nudged him jokingly in the ribs.

'This is no laughing matter, you two. Stop with the frolicking,' he said.

I thought, 'Oh, listen to the oh-so-clever one…'

'I heard that, Bud. You two, this is a serious matter and the change is a very dangerous time not only for Bud, but for us all,' said Stentorian. 'If you do not survive this, what will happen to our worlds and the throne, your throne? Have you forgotten who you are and all that rides on this?' he said sternly.

You never ever knew if he was being serious or fun as he never smiled, a trait unfortunately that stone creatures had not been born with.

'But do not worry. You are still eating, and because of this the change cannot and will not happen. It will only be triggered when you stop consuming calories, Bud,' Stentorian said. 'So you snuggle down.' And as he said this, he pulled up my covers and kissed me on the forehead.

As he reached my door, he turned and said, 'Nighty night.'
As the door was nearly shut, I called out. 'Stentorian?' I said.
'Yes?' he asked.
'Leave the light on.'

I stand in front of my full-length free-standing mirror. I look at myself. I have turned into not quite a butterfly but yet not human. I study myself and ask, what am I? How can this be? Am I a creature or a being? I stand in front of the mirror and I still resemble a human, but the pressure I feel on my head suggests otherwise.

I feel my hair and there are lumps that are coiled so tightly they make my head ache. I am fourteen now. I shout for Stentorian at the top of my voice when I notice something else… wings – and something poking out beneath my robe.

'Stentorian,' I shouted, feeling very light headed.

Suddenly, there he was, hovering in my bedroom doorway with a pinny around his middle.

'What on earth is going on… it is not time,' he said.

'Stentorian, just stop right there…' I said, holding my hand up to form a stop sign. 'Look at me.'

'I am looking! Oh my,' he said, as he hovered in the doorway before moving into my bedroom.

'Do not "oh my". Look at me, I look hideous,' I said to him.

'Metamorphose,' said Stentorian.

'Metamorphose?' I said.

'Yes. Metamorphose, Greek for the change Metamorphosis. The soup must have gone wrong. How you do feel?' asked Stentorian.

'What soup are you making and why is Hettie not cooking it?' I questioned.

'No, I am not making soup at all. Your soup,' he said.

Screwing up my face and raising my voice, I cried, 'My soup? How do you think I feel… feel tears? A range of hormones are swimming through my body so powerful that I feel trapped within it, it does not even feel like my body any more. I feel like something is taking over and I am fighting all these forces, not just outside here but inside there as well. I am not quite a butterfly but not yet human. What am I?' I covered my face with my hands, frustration taking over me.

'That's why the change is happening, it is how your species digests itself, we call it "the soup". While this happens, the soup transforms your eyes, wings, antennae and adult structure. But something has happened, the structure has gone wrong,' said Stentorian.

'What am I? How can this be?' I wailed in dismay. 'What has happened to me? Am I a creature? Or am I a being? I am not a caterpillar or a butterfly. The thing I currently most resemble is a roll of fat. So what, I am something between the two now?' I started to shake and quiver.

'I do not know what has happened but we will sort it,' said a calm Stentorian.

'But I am nearly a caterpillar!'

'No, a caterpillar you may never become, but for some strange reason you do have the attributes both of larva and a butterfly,' said Stentorian.

'But look, my backbone looks like that of a caterpillar. I have coils on my head and the pressure is immense,' I said. 'Why will I never become a caterpillar, have I never been one?'

'You will never become one, Bud. A caterpillar morphs into a butterfly. Your species has the attributes of the caterpillar but should not change into one at all,' said Stentorian.

'It is amazing, what is happening, but I am afraid,' I said.

'Formation of the chrysalis has gone horribly wrong and this is what the Butterfly Doctor was talking about. You have experienced the change but for some reason only parts of it have occurred. As we said, you are a unique species. I'm sorry to have to tell you this, but this will happen monthly.'

'Monthly...' I repeated, in a state of shock.

'Yes,' said Stentorian.

"You have got to be joking,' I said, snapping to attention and jumping to my feet, only to nearly fall to the ground.

'Careful,' said Stentorian, as he hovered over and helped me to get to the mirror, where I steady myself.

'Just look at me. And you say this will happen monthly? Oh, Lord help us all,' I said.

'Moulting has gone wrong.'

'You are telling me,' I said.

'Having two bodies within one, you haven't coped with the surge of hormones, causing them to knit together wrongly,' he said.

'Two bodies... so does that mean I have two souls?' I asked.

'Now that is a question. Where did that come from?' remarked Stentorian, surprised.

'I do not know where that came from, I just thought of it,' I said.

Standing in front of the mirror, I looked like a monster. Three species within one... I just could not get over the so called "change".'

Baby, child, juvenile, hormonal teenager, adult, Pupa, caterpillar, butterfly, shed skeleton, chrysalis emerging into half-human half-butterfly.

But reproduce I will not, as it would be too dangerous. I could crush my unborn child and myself, then who would save our worlds from colliding? Everyone would be left to face death alone and there would be no worlds left.

'I will help you to fix yourself, Bud,' said Stentorian.

'Do not despair, do not give up,' said Glitter.

I looked at Stentorian and Glitter.

"It is the forever changing of the three worlds. It's the bacterium.' I said.

'Yes, a microbe entering and causing a virus. Stentorian did not know what was happening to me but I would find that Tomes book in order to save and survive another day,' I said.

Chapter 10 – A Quest alone.

Another dawn was breaking and I had woken up to the reality of facing my quest alone. I sat back in my bedroom chair, which had its back to a skylight window. The window was open just a crack, to let fresh air in and stale air out from the night before. This had the added benefit of meaning I could hear anybody or anything making a noise and be alert at a moment's notice.

I had not slept again last night. If the truth be known I had not slept properly for days, no, come to think of it, weeks. It had been weeks since I had gotten a decent night's slumber, as Stentorian had been laying unwell on his stone bed for weeks, and I was too worried about him to sleep myself. Nobody knew what was wrong but Zena suspected the forever changing currents of the three worlds, an infection escaping in time. For whatever reason, Stentorian had fallen fowl to this bacterial organism. It was made even more unfortunate by the fact that it happened as I was experiencing my first change.

Gladstones, Greenlands and Blacklands, gosh were so obscure in every way, stood in different time zones.

I choked back the tears at the thought of losing my dearest friend, my mentor, my strength, my anchor and my stone. This time I would have to make my quest alone, I simply had no choice but to go it alone. I needed to get back to Greenlands as quickly and as fast as possible to collect a remedy for Stentorian for him to have any chance in hell. I had to stay mentally strong if I was going to get through this. I had to go if Stentorian had any hope of getting well again.

I sat back and just took a second to relax. It was astounding that I was going to fly on my own for the first time but I guess there was a first time for everything. I always knew this day would come, but I never imagined that it would be under these circumstances.

It was at this moment I heard the gaggle of geese, which zapped me out of my thoughts and back to the present. Hearing their honking made me smile. I smiled and looked over my shoulder towards the sound as I watched the geese fly higher and they honked to encourage each other to keep on going on their migration. I smiled and looked over my shoulder towards the sound. I knew the geese were pleased once again to be flying together. When they flew in a plump it looked like one gigantic bird, flying for victory, as they flew over the treetops and kept flying in 'v' formation.

I knew it was time for me to take flight too. I felt nervous but knew I had no choice; I had to do this, on my own. Yes, Glitter could have come but he had to keep twenty-four hour surveillance over Stentorian, there was no one else that had the knowledge to help him. Glitter would know exactly when to give him a cold compress, as giving him too many would result in him drowning in his own mucus. Glitter knew just as much as me, if not more, about stone creatures: how to manage him, how to handle him, how to sit for hours watching for any signs of darkness appearing around his crevices of stone and, most importantly, what not to do.

As I climbed onto the back of my chair, I perched on its back and turned around, taking one last look at my space, my room, my home. I felt a pull but then my body caught a little gust of air and I instantly turned around. The outside was pulling me towards the open sky, towards the unknown and my quest alone.

Looking through the crack of the skylight, my eyes darted from side to side, eager to escape. I now knew what a caged wild animal must feel like. My eyes scanned the sky, examining the conditions before I dared venture out.

I did not want any farewells, any goodbyes. The atmosphere in the house was heavy; everyone felt despondent knowing that I was going. I told them to go about their daily chores, ignoring the fact that I was going, but there was one being (he was a creature, actually) that felt my emotions and knew exactly when I was going to take flight. It was none other than... Stentorian. Even though he was terribly ill now, I knew he would be guiding me through our innermost thoughts. As I looked out over the rooftops, I felt apprehensive, but at the same time excited at the thought of swooping, shooting, sailing and darting through those billows above. Flitting, floating and fluttering, feeling totally free, was my favourite thing, especially when I flew parallel to the flight paths that took me home to Greenlands.

As my thoughts subsided, I squeaked through the crack of the window. Gosh, as I did so I thought that it was a bit of a squashy squeeze. Hmm, less sugar, less of those rotting banana skins coated in chocolate, I think. Butterflies do not eat chocolate, yes, but human beings do and as I was half-human half-butterfly, I had two treats in one. Whether it was good for me or not, I liked it. Gosh, I was always munching on those tasty rotting skins when I was changing. I knew I needed to eat more natural sugars but I was a herbivore and could not stomach protein, unlike my cousins, who loved protein (a hairy mantis never went amiss). I also needed less carbs but eating for one butterfly and one human was no easy feat. A trip to the Butterfly Doctor was needed, and I should probably start back at the gym... Just joking, as if I needed more exercise. I was always on the go.

I was now perched on my tiptoes on the rooftop, looking out across the great skies before me. I looked for the skein of geese but they were long gone, nowhere to be seen. As I looked through this vast wilderness, I knew the green, green grass of Greenlands was beyond the shining hours. I closed my eyes, breathed in through my nose (my human nose) and crouched into a ball. As

I let out my human breath, my butterfly breath took over and with this I came up and uncurled myself and stood tall. I could hear a humming and looked around but then I realised it was the sound of my wings fluttering, as they had emerged, craving to take flight. I started to hover up, and as I did, my wings opened and closed, stretching further each time, getting used to being used again. They flapped faster and faster, and before I knew it I was flying, aiming towards the furthest cloud.

'You go, Bud. Go, fly like the wind,' said Stentorian.

I smiled as I heard Stentorian's voice inside my head.

'I will fly like the wind, staying mighty strong' I said aloud.

The day was good for flying but as I flew higher there was a chill in the air. I knew I had to be careful not to go too high, as I knew the consequences of my actions if I became too cocksure. There was no sign of the geese anywhere and I could not hear them either, not even with my brilliant hearing. I wondered where they had gone.

It was a great feeling being up here and as I flew higher, I felt my confidence growing. But unfortunately, what goes up, must come down, and it was the coming down that took a little getting used to. I was terrified of heights – in training, all those years ago, it had taken a while for me to get used to, and even now fears came back to haunt me every once in a while. Suffering with vertigo and being aware of a need to descend did not go well together at all.

I enjoyed flying up to the height of the clouds, but what I enjoyed even more was flying *through* the clouds. The clouds looked like giant balls of fluff, almost like candy floss. I loved diving into them and disappearing into their bouncy bushiness.

I flew faster and faster, pushing myself further. I ascended to reach the highest cloud I could see, before descending as quickly as I could, feeling like a bullet being released from the barrel of a gun. The power as intense and I felt as if I was being released.

Now I could settle, as I had blown away the cobwebs from myself. I was flying towards Greenlands and had to focus on the task in wing. Stentorian had told me to look ahead at all times, looking out for the two peaks of the hills, as that was where I would have to land, which I must say I was not looking forward to, as I knew it was going to be a bumpy landing. Looking down as I flew, with the breeze constantly in my slits, I could hear nothing. Suddenly, there they were – straight ahead! I saw the tip of the peaks and so began to put the brakes on to slow myself down. As I came down, I flew between them, as Stentorian had instructed me to. Without this opening, I would never find my way back home. I didn't even want to entertain the thought.

Wow, I thought, as I flew between the peaks of the hills. I was so impressed by their height and beauty. Now, it was here that I was to hover, as instructed by Stentorian, and supposedly these great peaks would reveal to me what I needed to see to get into Greenlands. I had to look for the ridge in one hill which met with trees in the opposite hill that were parallel with each other. I looked and looked again and I knew this was where they were opposite to where the hills met. This was it, this was the opening and here was the path to enter Greenlands.

It was here that I was to land and make my way on foot.

As I came closer to the ground, I knew I was in for a bit of a battering on landing. I never had got this right and my technique was certainly in need of some practice. Luckily, there was plenty of soft, long grass, like a row of cushions, to soften the blow of my fall. As I came down, I stuck my feet out to use as brakes and steadied my wings to slow me right down to make the land as bump free as possible. 'Aaaaaaah!' I screamed, taking some small trees with me as I fell with a thud into the side of the hill. I had landed. At least I had wings which I was able to use as a parachute, which meant less bruising.

As I picked myself up, I dusted myself down. Gosh, grass stains were terrible, but nothing that a good old fashioned remedy from Doris or Betty couldn't sort out. As I walked through the grass, I collected my thoughts, picking them up and placing them into neat little boxes inside my head. No doubt they would come out later and be all muddled again, needing another mammoth sort out.

As I stood and looked all around me, I saw the fertile valley which led to the town of Greenlands, I could see for miles and looked out on the Great Plains, the prairie of the great green, green grasses of home. I closed my eyes and breathed in through my slits. The air felt good. If only I could bottle it, take it back and sprinkle it over Gladstones. The air was so very pure, clean, and fresh here – it made me feel brand new. I opened my eyes and walked down the hill, past the single tree, the medicine tree. I smiled as I walked past. I entered into the olive grove; nets were up ready for a bountiful harvest. Gosh, one thing I noticed straight away was the humidity, as Greenlands was tropical. It was so very warm! I would soon reach the right temperature here. As I climbed down, I could see great activity as it was low hours, which in Greenland's meant time was early as I entered Greenlands. As the heat of the day was at its lowest, this was the easiest time to get chores done, before the heat of the day made it unbearable to do anything. I smiled as I came down the hill into these great valleys before me, where I saw stone creatures and beings busy, bustling brightly at their tasks in hand. I was seen then disappeared as I turned a corner but when the corner disappeared I reappeared.

'Is that – was that Bud I saw?' asked Stoney.

'It sure was,' said Greystone. 'It sure was.'

As I came around the corner, everyone had gathered to receive me. Wow, I felt honoured. There were so many hows, smiling faces and hellos that soon everyone's voices became muffled into one, and I couldn't work out what anyone was saying. Beings were jumping up and down, insects were flying around my head and whoops, a little, tiny firefly got stuck in my hair. My hand came up to untangle a distorted, if not very disgruntled, baby firefly, but she was well and truly stuck.

'There, there, baby firefly, do not be so cross,' I said, using both hands to untangle her from my lengthy hair.

I could hear her buzzing loudly and alarmingly, but soothingly my fingers worked nimbly to free her. Her tail flashed alarmingly, as she disliked being held. Once I had freed her I held her in my hands and smiled thoughtfully, but she looked at me so unkindly. I pulled her in close and blew my breath over her, which turned into a thousand glistening stars.

Suddenly, there was a hush. This was never seen before by anyone, but to me it was just, well, it was my breath. They all marvelled in awe of this magical power I had but then I had many! I was unique, half-butterfly half-human, but you see I knew no different… or did I?

'You will instantly recover and be restored.' With this, I let the vivacious, flashing firefly go and she smiled sweetly, flying around my head. Any damage caused would have been magicked away by my thousand stars. But then, was it magic? It was just my breath. My power but power was only ever power in the right hands and with the right minds.

'You will make me vertiginous, flying around like this,' I said.

'And I will get a stiff, sore neck if I have to keep looking up to you,' said Stoney.

'Aha!' Bending down and kneeling on my knees, I smiled.

'Stoney, how are you?' I asked.

'I am well, thank you, very well, and all the better for seeing you home again.'

Stony grabbed me with his long, dangly arms and they wrapped around me twice. Stone creatures have such amazing flexibility with their limbs. Hard to believe, as they were rock solid and made of stone, but felt squidgy at the same time. Made up of so many different elements, their forms were mind-boggling structures. With their long, knobbly fingers and long, pointed nails too, they would be the most astonishing sight to you humans. Not to me, though, as I had known stone creatures all my life. I hugged him too. Looking down at his fingers, I said, smiling, 'Wow, Stoney, you so desperately need a manicure.'

'They will soon drop out and I will grow another nail plate,' he said.

'I know,' I replied. Yes, it may sound disgusting but that is exactly what happened to stone creatures' nails when they became long, hard, old and worn – they just grew another set. They simply grew black and would fall out of their fingers and they would grow another. Hence no manicure was ever needed here.

We both looked at each other. Stony was so like Stentorian in many ways, but then he was his father's son.

'How is Pop?' asked Stoney.

This reminder of Stentorian's condition hit me like a tonne of bricks. All of my happiness at being back home simply vanished into the very air I breathed. It was like being transported back in time, back to Gladstones, back to his stone bed, and all the emotions came flooding back.

I was still on my knees, so I could not hide any of my feelings. Stoney only stood four feet tall – he was only a stone creature after all.

'Stoney, it is merciless,' I said.

'No,' he said.

Those stone creatures showed no emotion but I felt his pain.

'I am so sorry,' I said.

He gripped his fingers into me tightly.

Greystone moved in as he realised the damage being done. I was being gripped hard by his grandson and little piercings had been made all along my arms and where my wings formed.

'Stoney, it is written,' said Greystone.

It was like he was in a trance. This is what happened when stone creatures needed to show emotion – they entered a trance like state.

'He is gravely ill. I have come to get the remedy he needs to have any hope in hell of surviving this bacterial organism,' I said. As I stood up, a single tear drop fell and dropped onto his cheek. As he looked up, he wiped it away. But as I turned to walk away, my hands slipped into his and I cried and I cried. I looked down to my side and he looked up at me. And even though stone creatures were unable to show emotion, I knew he felt pain, not only his own but mine too. As he looked at me, I felt liquid seep from the palms of his hands. These were his tears. He seeped liquid from every pore of his body and as I looked behind me he left a trail of tears.

'I am sorry I cannot tear too,' he said.

'Believe me, I wish I had been born with no emotion too,' I replied.

Before Stoney could reply, the silence was broken by the thud of a stone-edged stick hitting the ground and making me jump.

'Stop this! How can you say this, to be born with no emotion, have you lost sight of who you are, Buddy? I am cross – what would you prefer? To be born as an Evilliton, to live and be raised in Blacklands,' said Greystone.

'I... I... it has been so very tough,' I stammered.

'Tough, you have seen or felt nothing yet! Have you forgotten your hatch right and who you are?' he said.

'Maybe I have got lost again. Without Stentorian, I feel lost. I'm struggling to come to terms with not having him by my side,' I said.

I bent down and bowed, greeted this great solar. All Stentorian knew, he had learnt from his elder, his mentor, his pop, Greystone. We looked at each other, knowing each other's status. I smiled and he did too, in his own way.

'Come and sit down. Have some bog bean beer,' suggested Greystone. We sat down amongst the stones, where other stone creatures were ushered to get along with their business but advisors and elders sat amongst us. As we sat, we sipped from calyces made of stone, which helped to keep the bog bean beer cool from the rising temperatures and humidity.

'Grief is what you are feeling,' he said.

'Well, if this is what I am feeling, you can keep it. But surely grief is when someone has passed?' I asked.

But you are grieving the loss of a great friend who has been by your side for the last twenty years, Bud. And my, how the time has flown. You must learn to cope alone,' he said.

'Like my quest alone?' I asked.

'Yes,' said Stoney and Greystone together. 'Like your quest alone.'

'Cope, but have I not coped with enough?' I said, indignant.

'Cope. There is more to come. Your quest, I am afraid, has only just began,' said Stoney.

Greystone sat back, sipping his bog bean beer and smoking on his clay pipe to clear his thoughts. As he blew out the smoke, we watched the smoke form images of the early years. How much easier life had been before disaster and destruction had struck!

'You are in denial of his illness,' said Greystone.

'But am angry too,' I said.

'Bargaining will come into play, bargaining with your thoughts and how you could have done it better. If you had done this different,' he said.

'What do you mean, what could have I done better?' I asked. With my thoughts in full flow, Stoney said, 'It is time.'

'Yes, it is time to get the remedy. We must collect it before high hours, before it is too late,' said Greystone.

An elder looked up and chanted in Latin, 'Ante quod opaca noctis est super nobis. Venit, venit, lets facere festuna,' which translates to, 'Before the shadowy night is upon us. Come, come, let's make haste.'

I bowed and said 'vale', which translates to 'farewell' to my elders (I spoke Latin too, it was my mother tongue), who covered me in smoke to protect me.

I walked, while Greystone and Stoney hovered, away from the stones and up to the little hill where I walked through the olive trees to the place beyond, where one tree stood all alone. Here, Greystone and Stoney drilled their long, bony, knobbly fingers into the trunk of the tree. Then, as they pulled out the wooded plug, out came the finest golden sap that I ever did see, which they collected in little wooden calices, which translates to cups.

My mouth started to water. I loved this refreshment so much! All the trees at Gladstones in the woodlands were dry now and did not give any sap, but their sap would have been poisonous to Stentorian anyway. He needed sap from this tree, mixed with the liquid of evergreen tree bark, dew from the green grasses of home, beetle dung and a few other ingredients. The remedy was all prepared and finished before high hours. It was placed in little silver pouches, left from where baby caterpillars had laid in their chrysalis state and emerged into butterflies.

The silver pouches were passed to Pea and Pebble, who gracefully sewed through them with a silver needle and the purest silk from the silk worm. It was sealed, and the next being to open this silver pouch would be me, when I gave it to Stentorian.

'Thank you,' I said.

'You do not have to say thank you,' said Pebble. 'It is done with love.'

'Love is all around me. But why do I feel so alone?' I said.

I looked and Pebble, Stentorian's wife, Pearl, and babies, Bean, Pea, and Pip (the pebblets triplets had finally been born), Stoney and Greystone stood watching me. Their love for me may not be shown but I felt it.

I had now been here for two weeks in Greenlands time, but in Gladstones it would have only been a day or so. Time was nothing, but in Greenlands time was everything. It went so quickly it was frightening. The days here had wings on them.

'You must make haste. Come, let's walk to the market place and get you in place to pop back to Gladstones,' said Greystone.

'No' I said.

'What do you mean?' asked Greystone.

'It is okay, I will fly back to Gladstones,' I said.

'It is high hours now, Buddy, it is too late to fly,' said Greystone.

'I will be okay. I will be fine to fly.'

'There is a chill in the air. The weather is starting to turn for the worse and a blizzard is on its way, I feel' said Pearl. As she said this, she wrapped a piece of blanket silk around my shoulders having noticed me shivering slightly.

'Buddy, you are cold. Come on, it may affect your flight,' said Stoney.

'I will be fine,' I said.

So we all took a slow walk back up the hill, through the olive groves and to where the medicine tree stood alone and beyond.

I hated farewells at the best of times and knew I would be back soon but I knew that Greenlands time would pass so terribly quickly, and days would pass in Greenlands but be mere blinks of an eye in Gladstones.

'I bent down on my knees and embraced Stoney. Pebble took a piece of my silk blanket. They both stepped to one side, revealing Greystone, who stood looking forlornly at me.

'Here is the remedy,' he said and, as I lifted my wing, he tucked it into my pouch, doing up the popper. I lowered my wing and he patted it down.

'Keep it so very safe. Guard it with your life,' he said.

'I will,' I said, reassuring him.

I bowed and as I did so I started to hover up. My wings opened and started to flap, and before I knew it I was gone. My return flight started well, some parts of my journey took me out of my flight path and at some points it became so windy that it was like being in a washing machine, being blown from left to right, right to left, in a drum. I struggled hard to keep my balance, but just as I began to feel in control again I was swirled, spun, and rolled around again. I suffered quite a lot of turbulence! It was not easy and the weather certainly had changed.

As the moon rose, it gave me light at least to see where I was going. The moon lit up the earth below me, reminding me that it was an ideal night for a hunt, and suddenly I was starving hungry. I remembered that the Butterfly Doctor had told me that the monarch butterfly hunted this way and it would be good for me to shadow a hunt, to show me how the big boys hunted. But there was no time – I needed to enter Gladstones sooner than later.

I looked down and could see dew balls glistening in the moonlight. I felt weak after leaving Greenlands, but I knew I must continue this quest alone.

Then the weather changed dramatically, and I was flying frantically against a bitterly cold icy rain now and the flight became very hazardous. I knew I was getting into a sticky situation and I needed to end this flight. I could feel the sudden drop in temperature. Oh no, I saw the ice building up on the tips of my wings. I saw the cloud formation had changed and there was no moon now so now I was flying in the pitch black, completely dark, as black as pitch. I could feel and hear the rain; it felt as if it were turning into sleet and gosh, those small frosty balls of ice hurt! Then it turned into snow, tiny crystals of light flakes, which I much preferred. It suddenly started to build thicker and heavier – a blizzard was forming! I knew flying was going to be an impossible task.

I was also now becoming too cold and my body I knew was not above eighty-six degrees. I needed to be this temperature to be able to fly. I knew I had been foolish by going against what Greystone had said. Pearl had also said the weather was on the change and I had flown for far too long. I had suffered a lot of turbulence by fighting against high winds before the rain. I was simply becoming too exhausted to fly anymore.

It was so very dark now and I was suddenly wondering how I was going to manage to get back to Gladstones, if at all.

But then, I remembered who I was. I was the child prodigy of Zena and I was not going to allow anything to let her down or the stone creatures and beings of my worlds. This remedy was going to get back to Gladstones even if I did not make it.

Exquisite, sensitive eyes which normally allowed for my navigation were not working now and a haze had built up – or was it frost over my lens? I started to spiral out of control. I think I had now lost my senses as one by one they were disappearing. As I was losing consciousness, I bumped into something. My eyes were closed but I could sense a dark shadow, and it was large too. With the last ounce of strength I had left I opened my eyes; it was the Monarch Butterfly. Or was it angels? Had I now entered the dark side of heaven? I knew the angels would come if I got into danger.

I thought I was going to land with a splat. I have no idea what happened, but one moment I knew I was in terrible danger and the next thing I knew I had fallen on the Gladstones. I was so very cold. Where was I? I thought and then looked and saw my hands I was human again – I could feel no wings and I was laying down on my side. I had been placed on Gladstones, back in the warmth. I was back home, but the bitterness of the cold, solid slab of stone hitting my body as I had fallen was like being placed on a mortuary slab. I smiled but was shivering so much that I closed my eyes to try to escape my reality. Suddenly, my cousins appeared and I was covered in a blanket... a blanket of butterflies... they laid on me to keep me warm, to protect me from the bitterly cold elements. It was at this extremity that I felt the first snowflake of the first falls of snow and stuck out my tongue. But it was not my human tongue, but my butterfly one. I felt a pain which was so intense that I could focus on nothing else. I felt as if I was on fire. It was in my last moments of consciousness, before the pain overwhelmed me, that I caught sight of a dark, hovering figure standing over me. This was when I closed my eyes.

Chapter 11 – Zena.

Zena was a sensation and a flop. What can I say, each time I set eyes on her I was in complete awe. I mean, after all this while I assumed I knew her. You know, I thought I knew her so very well, but in fact I did not know her at all. I mean, it takes a lifetime to truly know someone right. As I looked up at her now, I thought there were so many layers to her, it was like peeling an onion with her. There was so much depth to her that I had barely scratched the surface. I was still intrigued to know about her, every time I got a little closer to knowing her a little more it was then time for her to take flight again to flutter away. This was the flip-side to her being so sensational. This did make me feel dejected and yes, frustrated. Now I remember why M cried so when Zena flew away! I mean she was a queen of such status who reigned several worlds.

Then I had learnt the secret that she was actually my biological mother. It was like a bittersweet chocolate, difficult to swallow and with a nasty aftertaste. Yes, I was me, but this time it was hard to take on board, hard to consolidate two mothers from two different worlds... But, no matter how many books I read or how many questions I asked Stentorian, without her, I certainly would not be here! At times I was cross at my hatch date and coming to terms that one day all the problems of the worlds would be on my shoulders, but for certain I could say she was a fine specimen of her race, which I still did not understand to this day. Half-insect, half-human, it was quite bizarre.

I was still learning what I was, what I had become – half-human, half-insect and perfectly perfect in every way! I did wonder why after all these years she was still alone, but Zena was abandoned by her mother as a caterpillar – my species do not abandoned their babies! Yes, my cousins are reared this way but we were not and would not have survived such a fate. Zena had found it so hard to accept happiness and let it in. She had many issues, she had grown to fear such a lot and it had taken her from girl to woman to sort it all out, or should I say from larva to adult butterfly. The opposite sex – Zena did not understand their needs and what they could possibly want from her. I knew for certain, Zena felt very much alone and often had unfathomable feelings of loneliness. So many beings, humans and insects around her, so many friends and family that loved her, but in the end nobody could dispel the loneliness she felt. At times, even when there was a roomful of beings around her, I knew she felt so very much alone. Zena. I knew she was prepared to isolate herself rather than be with the wrong being. She could not settle for anyone lesser than her.

Thinking and looking back through my mind maps, I do believe, once, I am almost certain, I witnessed a conversation between my mother and my father. It took place while I was sleeping… yes, I know I was meant to be sleeping. As I looked back through the passages of my mind, I remember hearing a male's voice and it was no other voice I have heard before. It was written that I would hear him but never see him. The King, my father. Zena was speaking to my father… it was when I had to leave Gladstones and visit Greenlands and my kind to understand more about where I came from. As I hear I can automatically record conversations and it went a little like this:

'Wow, Zena, is this really where I live? Seeing Greenlands for the first time was truly magnificent in every way, as magnificent as Gladstones but in a different way. I was trying to think how they were different, but then realised Gladstones was surrounded by moorland and stones, yet Greenlands was an old market town surrounded by countryside, as the name suggested. Green, so very green. Grass everywhere, trees and plants and warm with a tropical climate, but so very green as a lot of rain fell throughout the year.'

'Yes, Buddy, this is really where you come from,' said Zena.

'Then why did I need to be adopted by their Lord and Ladyship?' I asked.

'You ask this so many times,' she said, as she fluttered up, and, bending down, Zena tickled my tummy with her proboscis while I was in my cocoon bed.

'On your hatch day, Greenlands became unsafe to raise you and our enemies, the Evillitons, wanted you to pass,' she said.

'But why, Zena, why? If I were to pass I would surely never reign, I would be no longer. I have no desire to hurt them,' I said.

'Darling, I know you would not hurt them, but they do not see the world as you do, in a harmonious bubble. Unfortunately, the world is full of wealth, beauty and...' Zena looked at me (her daughter) for the answer.

'Wealth and beauty in turn breed contempt, greed, envy and pain.'

'Well done, you are learning fast, but we still have so much to teach you.'

It was at this very moment Zena stopped and stared out into the open space. It was as if she was in a trance, being mysteriously pulled out into the open. All was quiet now. Suddenly, she collected her thoughts and, turning her head to look back, said, 'Wait here, there is someone I need to speak to. You must wait here.'

Of course I did not wait there, when did I ever do as I was told? Besides, that was so mind numbingly boring for an eight-year-old, don't you think?

I followed Zena out to an opening and then down a steep rocky terrain… I had to be careful not to miss my footing on the small shards of loose slate that lay in my path and did not want the noise of them underfoot to give away my presence. But, you know, Zena had a sixth sense, like me, and if she concentrated hard enough she would know I was following her. I always had the power to see in so many ways, which is how I always kept myself out of danger as an infant. As I followed her, the small, steep path came down into an overgrown oasis, which seemed like a perfect place to rendezvous. I had to keep hidden and all I could see was Zena's back, but now and again, I got a shimmer and could hear what sounded like two pieces of metal clinching together. Somebody's armour, perhaps? Every now and then, I caught a glimpse of a shadow, a tall, dark stranger, which I now believe was my father. As my mother spoke, I heard her say:

'Do not ever say I walked away. I will always want you, but I had to walk away... I feel broken. My emotions have broken me,' cried Zena.

'Zena, no... I will not allow you to walk away. I will give up all I have to be with you, please.'

'You are married! Besides, there is not just only me,' she said.

'Zena,' said my father.

I was shocked. How this could be my father, a wife, a Queen and me. Gosh, sometimes it is better to know nothing than to know everything. I felt betrayed by this tall, dark stranger who stood before my mother, but also I felt I had betrayed the Queen by not listening. I now knew the truth of his existence... I had followed her, not realising at the time, but realising very quickly now, that I had put myself in danger yet again, great danger. I was soon about to learn a very good lesson about what happens when we break rules. I became suddenly aware of my parents having a heated discussion.

I heard my mother say, 'Everything happens for a reason.'

'You must go, the Evillitons are here. Let me help you,' he replied, tensely.'

'"Help", I remember the last time you said that word to me. You left me in egg and you now you want to help me. All of the eggs perished... 'said my mother, trying to hold back tears.

'What eggs, what are you talking about?' asked my angry father.

What a mistake it was to get so deeply concentrated into a conversation that seemed to be going nowhere. As I turned around, the shadows were here... the Evillitons were encroaching on me. I stood tall, trying to hide the fear that was coursing through my body, and called, called with all my might.

'ZEEEEEEEEEEEEEEEEENA!'

'But one survived,' said my mother, not hearing me.

'What do you mean, one survived? Zena, we have a baby caterpillar? he asked.

'Yes, one did, and I will do everything in my power to make sure she reigns as the greatest queen!' she said.

'A daughter – I have a daughter?' he asked.

'I won't allow her life to be put in danger,' said Zena.

At that moment a clap of thunder was heard by the king and queen.

'You have never wanted to help before.'

'Clap of thunder,' they both said.

'No, you do not have a daughter. I do,' said Zena fiercely.

'Zena, help me!' I screamed out.

'Wait, I can hear Buddy over the sound of the thunder,' said Zena.

In unison my parents said, horror dawning on them, 'Evillitons.'

'Wait, Buddy is with the Evillitons!' Zena panicked.

'Wait, who is Buddy?' asked my father, slow on the uptake.

'Wait, for what? What, you want her to perish to like the rest of our brood? Zena questioned.

'Zena, no,' my father said.

The smell was putrid, filling the air. Their faces were harrowing, and as they opened their mouths to snatch my smile, the stench of sulphur left their mouths and entered mine. It was intoxicating. With the smell, came the loudest clap of thunder I had ever heard.

How I hated the smell, which clogged up the whole of my thorax, making it impossible for me to breathe. I was not yet mature enough to cope with the fumes... They seeped into every part of my skin, which no doubt caused the damage which made my puberty so difficult. I had no way to defend myself, I was far too small. Then, the wind picked up suddenly and it became so cold, so quickly, that my arms started to ache. It felt like I had the flu.

I started to cough and, without me realising, Zena flew right in front of me. Her glare cut straight through me, like a knife gliding through a piece of meat. If looks could kill, she would have struck me down on the spot. Zena turned and faced the massive problem in front of her. From behind, my mother spun silk thread around me which made a protective layer of film as she embroiled me in her under wings. Zena rose and we seemed to blend into our background.

The air was dense with clouds and the wind got up as I saw the trees blow. It became cold as condensation started to appear on the protective shield that my mother had cocooned me in. Gosh, I was cold as the shock set in but, being cocooned with in my mother's wings, I was at least safe. To think that this day started out to be so sunny and warm and now it was so dull, and gloomy, full of these moving shadows. When they got close enough, you could make out faces, but these faces showed no emotion. In fact, they appeared to be hollow faces, faces of living, walking corpses. Such a terrifying sight, one that I did not want to see again, but one I would though definitely.

'Take a good look, Buddy.' At this point, I shielded my face. The Queen moved my hand and guided my face out to take a look. Harsh, you would think, for an eight-year-old, but not an eight-year-old who had been raised to learn and conquer one world, and to keep another two safe. So I knew I had to know everything while my mother had the time to teach me. I had to learn fast...

'Take a good look at the evil, because these are our enemy. They come to drain every last piece of emotion from us. Bleed us dry, taking our emotion for themselves.'

'How do they, Zena?' I asked.

By drowning us in the shadows, in their shadows. They would suffocate us with fumes, like the smog of London. As they suffocate us, they would snatch our smiles, keeping them for themselves. Remember, I have always told you to stay away from the shadows,' said Zena.

The Evillitons were like the wind, really, like a depressing, lifeless, hungry cloud. But as they came closer, you could see a flicker of an expression of a goul, with no eyes, which somehow still managed to catch your gaze. This was their motive to take our expression as they had no face, no smile of their own.

On wrapping me in her wings, Zena rose into the air. It was so windy up there, there were gusts of up to 100 miles per hour swaying, swinging and shaking us from side to side – it felt like being in the drum of a washing machine. The turbulence was awful, but this was no ordinary wind and I knew, even at eight, that it was not due to normal weather conditions. It was evil, evil at its worst; it was the Evillitons.

Stentorian had taught me from a very young age about evil, though I knew no harm would come of me as long as the Queen wrapped me in her wings. It was very important that I remained entirely cocooned, as any knock would almost certainly be fatal, as it could damage my later development.

Goodness gracious! Golly me, her wings were amazingly soft, smooth, supple and silk – on the outside they were built as hard as an armadillo's shell, yet the insides were as soft as the finest silks from India.

As Zena rose, she attached herself to the bough of a tree, where we stayed while we waited for the Evillitons to disappear. I did not dare say a word, but knew what she was thinking. We just had to sit out the storm until they gave up their rant rage raved and calmed right down. It was a waiting game, but I knew I was in for it once I was unwrapped!

I must have fallen asleep because the next thing I knew, I felt a rush of air and knew I had been unwrapped, Zena was extremely careful and had not quite landed but had decided that her precious cargo deserved a rude awakening.

'It is no good, Buddy, you glaring at me. Do you realise how close we came to losing you today? You have no idea at the amount of trouble we were in, do you?'

'They, who are they?'

'We,' she stammered.

The Queen had not realised what she had said and did not quite know how to answer.

'When I say stay put, I mean stay put,' she said.

'What was that anyway? I asked.

'What was what anyway – what do you mean?' she replied.

'You know who I mean. Who was the man you were talking to?'

Zena looked at me with an icy stare. 'I will not discuss this any further. Evil, Buddy... through and through, pure evil. This is a time to think about how we can prevent situations like this from happening again.'

With this, she turned in disgust and walked away. Zena could not look at me all evening and did not speak either to me. Boy, she was mighty cross – I would say fuming!

In the morning, I woke up and could not get out of my cocoon bed. Actually, come to think of it, I could not move at all. I had this icky-like sticky substance all over my cocoon. I was trapped in my very own tomb. Try as I might, I was entombed, going nowhere fast. I was well and truly stuck.

I heard a loud flutter which indicated that Zena had arrived home.

'Did you sleep well, Buddy?'

'I am stuck, I think.' With that, I heard Zena sigh.

'I know you are,' my darling mother said. Try as I might, I was going nowhere fast.

'Really, cast your mind back to yesterday, Buddy.'

'You can wriggle as much as you like, but my glue will only weaken and allow victims to leave if and when I decide.'

'I do not understand, why am I your prisoner?'

'I will do everything in my power to keep you safe from harm…'

'Oh, for goodness sake, Zena! Let me go!'

'Do not be silly. You cannot be trusted, and until you can, when I take flight, I will entomb you, for your own safety.'

I looked at Zena with disgust, really angry that I was not getting my own way yet again, but try as I might, I was well and truly entombed, as Zena put it. I felt a sudden sympathy for a housefly caught in a spiders' web.

'I promise I will do as I am told.'

'Buddy, I know what you are thinking. You can promise all you like, my darling, but they are unopened promises that become broken.'

'What do you mean by unopened and broken promises?'

'Exactly that. There is no point in promises if they are opened up and then are broken. A promise is opened and once opened must not be left broken. An opened promised is half a promise wished and must be fulfilled and followed through to the end.'

I found myself totally in awe of this beautiful woman. She was in her human form when she was facing me, yet as she turned her back to me she switched to her insect form. Little did I know, I was looking at what I would myself become ten years later; half-human, half-insect.

Born at a time when peace overwhelmed my kind in Greenlands, my mother's upbringing was exceptionally privileged. Well, she was a princess, after all. Getting to know her was hard, and it was difficult coming to terms with what I was, let alone the fact that I had two mothers and a father. Nothing was ever said about him, nothing at all. My real father that is, not His Lordship. When I did approach the subject, it was almost like Zena's heart had had a close shave with a piece of ice. I had come to understand that my parents, my species, were of a prevailed state.

I needed to know more about my biological father if I was to understand the worlds which were in front of me. In order to understand my worlds: their beginning, their existence, and their unknown tomorrow. Surely, I needed to know about my personal heritage, in order to survive and safe another day.

I could not be everyone's heroine if I did not know all I needed to help my kind to survive in these vile times.

Chapter 12 – Evillitons.

What could I say about pure evil, which I never understood and had never learnt to understand? It had been a hard lesson to understand as I never ever saw wrong in any being, bad, I simply had not understood badness. Stentorian was a great professor, advising me that I would find what I needed, as I read I would understand more. It was beyond my thought processes, how any being could be so evil. All I knew was that they took all that was good, turned it bad, and threw it out again, in any being's direction. The Evillitons wanted what butterfly beings were, creatures too, and then I found out that humans had a similar genetic set up – emotion. If that was not enough, they wanted what human beings had too? The Evillitons wanted what they simply could never have; emotion. But they did not understand their actions, which spread sorrow, doom and gloom. They took beings' smiles and collected them, keeping what was not theirs to keep. They had many baskets full of smiles, and had tried many ways to wipe the smiles on their faces but there was no way the smiles would stay in place. I mean, why would they want to stay? All they were trying to do was hide all the sorrow of their own creation.

Evillitons lived at Blacklands, another world running parallel to one side to the worlds of Greenlands and Gladstones. Our kind have always known of the strange land caught in the middle of our worlds, but have never thought too much about the goings on there. When they came and started to take and never give back, that was when our kind started to fight back. This was not in our nature, but it was foretold from Elders present and past – the stories were told and the script was written on the wall, telling of the pure evil that lived beside us. I never wanted to know, and as an infant, I would cover my slits to not listen to the stories being told. Sadly, I had to be taught from a very early age about Blacklands. Even when I was in the cradle, Stentorian's stories would begin, but I was never scared and knew I had to listen. It was necessary, to learn and to protect my kind, and to help me build an even bigger force, to stop them colliding into us, to build stronger worlds for generations to come. I knew I had no choice if my kind was going to survive. No life seemed to exist there, because every last ounce had been picked up and had the life totally sucked out of it. Anyone who found themselves in their clasp was left a shadow of their former self, if they survived Evillitons' ordeal at all.

No one ever really knew when they were going to be faced with the evil but I knew signing heavily, that goddamn birth right. The coldness first made me sit and stare. The wind for me sent a shiver down my exoskeleton, and another one down my human spine. This was as good a sign as any and caused the word *hover* to spring into my head, telling me to wrap myself up and blend into the nearest background. The world as I knew it would change completely, the destruction that they left behind would fill you with hatred, and just wanted to make me cry. The wind would suddenly get up from nowhere and start dancing, howling like a wolf calling for its pack to come hunting.

The day would appear dismal, dank and dull. All beings first thoughts were to hide but sometimes to hide could be fatal. The thunder would start, though, of course, that was never a concrete sign, as it could just be normal weather. Certain claps of thunder would bring dark shadows, but in a cloud formation that danced and swirled around you. The Evillitons did not always show themselves, as they knew that we were aware of the signs of their arrival. They only appeared so as to size up the infirm, elderly, young beings or stone creatures at first but I knew this was pointless as stone creatures did not smile but then they had so much emotion which was what this pure evil wanted. The Evillitons concentrated on the strong beings.

The Evillitons were hideous to look at and if any beings were unfortunate enough to be caught, the stories told were always the same. Sunken, colourless faces, with empty sockets for eyes and a mouth that only opened ever so slightly at first, but then their entire jaw would drop open to catch a smile. Their mouth was empty, as they had no teeth, not even any gums for them to sit on... so they could not even form a smile. Forever angry, full of angst. Worse still, if they did not get what they wanted ... they would leave their vital mark, the ground scorched behind them.

I had many defences to protect me and could protect many if they were near enough. I was able to wrap my wings around my two bodies whenever I felt threatened, my wings automatically becoming my armour, as hard as steel. Like a knight in battle, I was protected with what I had fought against for so many years. As quick as the armour came, I would start to rise and blend into any background, using it as my camouflage if I had time. Time was not always on my side, however. Very often it was against me.

The Elders could never understand why they could see into our worlds, as they had no eyes to see –how did they know what they wanted if they could not even see it? Me, being the saviour, I had the task of finding out more, which is exactly what happened when I came across one great story which was etched on a wall while playing one day. I read it and it went a little like this:

It was written how one being from one world, Blacklands, had fallen in love with another being from my world, Gladstones. Their love for one another was forbidden by their families, as not only could the two species never be together, but the male's family had already chosen him a suitor. He did not want to marry the female his kind had chosen, but there was no way out. The male had spent his life liking too much flesh, then had been put in the path of a female he should have never been with. But, alas, the path had been set. For the first few months, all was well, but as time passed and they settled into a routine, he became bored and realised his mistake. I knew the female was simply not his match, he was not compatible with her. Yes, they had done things together, but we all can do things together with the opposite gender. They were not compatible sexually, so it simply was not going to work.

No amount of binding together was going to make it work, but his mother, his family in general, pushed them together. He went for the easy life; she became his security blanket and he could be king and a Walter Mitty in the imaginary world he lived in, but to him this was not reality. He walked around in his finery, playing the role of a king, but he talked to other females, slept with them too. Was he happy? No, and neither was she. Then, she wanted a baby. He did too, and so a child was made. It's just a shame that he made it with the wrong woman. All was well for the first six months of the infant's life, but then the cheating and the deceit happened began again. Eventually, the male thought he could live two lives, one with the mother of his child and one on the weekends, where he could continue to be himself, and explore flesh, have excitement, but it did not go to plan. His friend met a woman and became very happy and then the King met female with whom he got on so very well, was compatible with in every way. Unfortunately, he forgot to tell her his plan – to live two lives.

The story fades away and I found it difficult to read. It picks up again, saying how he fell in love with a unique species, a wonderful, delightful, sexy female but at the wrong time. Still, the secret, after nineteen months, could be taken no more by the female. She too had fallen in love, never expecting to after never being loved in childhood, never having felt loved at all. The female had found what she truly desired all her life – love, but still she could not have this man that she finally felt at ease with and able to conquer this world with, as he said he could not have his son and the woman he loved too. So, he chose his son, and to live under the same roof as the mother, just so he could be a father to his child. What woman could put up with that?

I had to stop reading as tears had formed on my lens and the tears had blurred my vision. It was so very sad; all this female's life she had never felt loved, had been soul searching for the one all this time, she finally falls in love and the male feels the same but then they are told they cannot be together. How heart breakingly sad. I gulped, as I could not read any more.

I sat and stared at the lands in front of me, but knew I had to find out more, to try to discover what happened to this female and male. If it was true love, then surely love would conquer all, but also religion played a big part in everyone's destiny and I could not help thinking there was more to this story.

The male loved her so, and did not believe in "the one", but seemed unsettled. He became tired of keeping everyone happy, tired of the double life, but then we, I believe, are in control of our destinies. We are dealt a hand of cards or put on a path, a crossroads – do we go right, left, or straight on? This is the million-dollar question.

So, as I followed the pictures, I saw tears from his eyes. Gosh, I thought a male was not meant to show emotion. You know, in all this time I had never ever seen a human being cry. Their kind was bought up by their mothers to be big and strong. To cry was a bad thing, but I felt this was negative, as sisters of their species were allowed to cry. I thought it somewhat a peculiar trait to be bestowed upon one.

He was angry and depressed, the combination of which led him to a frightening conclusion: if he could not be happy, then why should anybody else be allowed to be? He could not have the woman that he had fallen in love with and so, if he could not have her and have a smile on his face, then nobody else should.

Thereafter, each child born a son was stripped of emotion, a chromosome was removed and generation after generation of Evillitons were born. The Evillitons became the weaker race, and he was forced to observe how happy the neighbouring worlds were. One day he was walking aimlessly within his colony when he came up with the idea that if he stole our smiles, his kind would become a united race of strong beings again, living in harmony with other beings. But it was no good, the damage had been done, as his kind had evolved so that they were incapable of showing emotion.

How so very sad indeed, that because of all his greed, deceit the many lies he told, and his liking of flesh, he had inflicted his sorrow onto his own kind. The beings knew no different, born into a world of hate, disruption and deceit.

I was going to get to the bottom of this narrative but I knew this would take me on many quests for the truth to be found and eventually told. It was going to take me a lifetime to conquer, but I would get there in the end. I was not going to give up on my hatch right, my namesake and my true destiny to be everyone's saviour. There were going to be many battles to fight but I would win, I would fight to take over all the powers of my three worlds, to save my kind and the human beings too.

Love is a powerful emotion.